Edward S. Creamer

Adirondack Readings

Volume 5

Edward S. Creamer

Adirondack Readings
Volume 5

ISBN/EAN: 9783337181963

Printed in Europe, USA, Canada, Australia, Japan

Cover: Foto ©Andreas Hilbeck / pixelio.de

More available books at **www.hansebooks.com**

ADIRONDACK READINGS

BY

EDWARD SHERWOOD CREAMER

AUTHOR'S EDITION

BUFFALO

CHARLES WELLS MOULTON

1893

TABLE OF CONTENTS.

ADIRONDACK
READINGS.

ADIRONDACK READINGS.

PROLOGUE.

IT was the time of year when flowers were blown,
　When grass and small fruit were to ripeness
　　grown;
When farmers had just taken in the hay,
And golden wheat, for store or market day,
That on a road that entered the North Woods,
Through travel had been stopped by Nature's
　　floods
Having in tumult washed away the piers
Of rugged stone, which stood so firm for years,
Taking its wooden road-bed down the stream,
Dashing, like jumping fish, each board and beam—
To take the journey where the Hudson roams
Its shining foot-steps by a million homes.
　Here, at this stream, the stage-coach halting
　　came;
The passengers at first desired to blame,
While not a few with somewhat crossness spoke,
Who afterwards enjoyed it as a joke.
And, as the stream could not be bridged just then,
Some time for hewing timber, getting men,
Causing a delay of at least two days,
The pushing driver turned about his bays,

Taking his load of passengers back a mile,
Where a snug tavern rose in rustic style,
Furnishing good living to every guest.
Where food might be obtained cooked to request.
The house looked roomful, had a cheery face,
Was well located for the trout or chase.
The house itself, looking at its outside,
Was not as handsome as where many bide.
Its architecture honest, not too fine,
But strong and rugged in its bold outline
In the wood clearing, o'er against the sky,
Beside a brook unconscious babbling by.
A sort of wigwam with a gothic dome,
Made by an Indian, maybe, who saw Rome,
Was the quaint porch which hid the outer door,
Having board benches and an earthen floor.
The glass within the windows were kept clean,
On which nice snowy curtains could be seen;
While at one casement cut-flowers met the eye,
Lending their beauty to the passer by.
Three chimneys gave to it a warm attire,
Three high and bold to save the house from fire;
In winter, when the winds howled sharp and cold,
Their ample hearths would have what wood they'd
        hold.
Stables and barns were many and were large,
Kept neat and wholesome by those having charge;
Accommodating from the storm and rain
The horses, cows and fragrant hay and grain.
    The stage, which now had stopped before the
        door,
Contained eleven passengers or more;
As the good driver, country bred and tall,
Felt himself in companionship with all.

One was a woman, of the comely age,
Like a fair vision stepped she from the stage.
The other ten were made of sterner stuff,
Were Adirondack tourists sure enough.
Alighted safely they, without ado,
Taking their hand bags, some straps had a few,
And all of them had baggage on the way,
To surely reach them at a later day.
Some hurried in the house as best they could;
Some gazed upon the buildings, stream and wood,
But soon the rain poured down in torrents din,
When they too sought their neighbors who were in.
We will not here make question how they got
The money for this tour—one owned a yacht—
Enough for us to know that they were here,
With self esteem enough to banish fear.

Within the spacious room, where all were soon,
Was where the wayward traveler found a boon,
As cosy chairs invited each to rest,
Bringing a quiet to the troubled breast.
The fireplace ample was like those of old,
At which our fathers sat in winter cold;
Now, as the air was damp from fall of rain,
Some lengths of hickory blazed and did complain.
The mistress of the house was fat and fair,
Wearing in wavy curls her flaxen hair;
Good nature spoke in all her rounded form—
'Tis said she had a heart to suffering warm.
The host himself was tall, and straight, and spare,
With skin of saffron hue, and swarthy hair.
A radical he was, yet in his mind
He treated old forms fairly well and kind.
Jolly he was, and yet a moderate feeder,
And in the cool months an omniverous reader.

The maid-of-all-work's face was rubescent
From her high living, it was said, since Lent,
Which left her with its seal, this rosy face,
Seeming beyond her knowledge to erase.
It might be that the heat from kitchen fire
Brought out this redness, more than we'd desire;
Yet she made dishes which might well commend,
And he who loved good cooking was her friend.
The man-of-all-work, who split up the wood,
Was short and thickset, over full of blood;
Yet work could he from dewy morn till eve
Without a groan, or any thought to grieve;
The embodiment was he of living joy—
Looking as if he were less man than boy.
The waiting girls about the house were three.
Freshness itself, and artless modesty,
Spoke in the peachy bloom upon each face—
Bespeaking that they were of Northern race,
Where people have four months or more of snow,
Working with nature as a friend and foe.
    The house was built for more of use than show,
With sleeping rooms above, and rooms below
Where rational pleasure and good-will could thrive,
Built for the people who are now alive.
The bed-room walls were tinted modestly,
And on the floors nice matting could you see,
While beds and bedding were kept aired and sweet
Giving unto each sleeper a rich treat.
Bars of light netting filled each window frame,
To keep the insects of the air from blame.
Comfort and Peace reigned jointly in the house—
Crickets outside, and absent seemed the mouse.
    The room in which our travelers found a rest
Was doubtless seen the tavern at its best.

This room was wainscoted some four feet high,
Done in black walnut and maple—bird's eye—
Glazed o'er with something which gave it a gloss
Like what at times is seen on forest moss.
Upon the walls hung paper somewhat haze,
Containing figures grouped in various ways;
Dragons which looked from out of greenly eyes;
Monsters with mouths of more than monster size;
Eagles with tails which would a lion shame;
Lions with wings that would an eagle tame;
But over all the eye could plainly see
There was a look of graceful harmony;
And gentle shades filled all the pattern out,
And what one well could see one could not doubt.
The ceiling had a tinge of yellow white,
The mantle shelves were high and fair to sight.
The floor was walnut and white mountain ash;
In wintry months 'twas covered o'er with crash;
Now in the summer it was bare and clean,
With no rich rug its chasteness to demean.
    The pictures on the wall were few but rare,
Painted in colors with much taste and care.
The mantle held an Ecce Homo choice,
That well might make the pure in heart rejoice.
One of the walls held Lincoln's honest face,
And Osawatomie Brown's an opposite place;
While Thomas Paine smiled from another frame,
Near that large man George Washington by name.
The centre table held a statuette
Done by John Rogers—it is history yet—
And made a group containing figures four.
One a black woman, who's a slave no more.
Who nestles to her breast her timid child,
A fugitive from law at which men smiled.

One is John Whittier the poet true;
One is Lloyd Garrison a hero too;
One is Ward Beecher, who with words could charm—
This one by accident has lost an arm.
Upon the table, round this drab-toned cast,
Were princely books, bespeaking a great past.
The Bibles of the Christian and the Jew,
With the Al Koran, were in easy view.
And Bryant's Homer held an honored place;
And Chaucer, bard of old, with early grace,
Was beside Spenser's book of Faerie Queen,
While Sidney's Poesy was placed between.
Will Shakespeare and Ben Jonson blessed the board.
Near which was Webster, Massinger and Ford;
While Beaumont and Fletcher, and Kit Marlowe,
Were close to Drayton, Otway and to Rowe.
And Milton, for whom Zeus might risk a world
To see such genius in this life unfurled,
With Dryden, Pope, Parnell, Collins and Gray,
Were nigh to Coleridge, and Drake's Culprit Fay.
And Cowley, Goethe, Longfellow and Holmes,
With Johnson, Marvel, Beattie were by tomes
Of Goldsmith, Byron, Shelley, Moore and Scott—
Their nice rich bindings worn by use somewhat—
While Schiller, Halleck, Wordsworth, Thomson, Poe,
And Tennyson, and Dante, and Tasso,
With Beranger of France, with singing brain,
Were beside Motherwell, Bob Burns and Swain.
And the two Brownings, Campbell, Keats and Hood,
Beside the works of writers also good,

With Stedman, Stoddard, Howells, Whitman,
    Saxe,
And Bayard Taylor, Aldrich, Gilder, tax
With Joaquin Miller, Lowell, Mark Twain, nooks
Of other shelving, made for newer books.
Each corner of the room held walnut frames,
Filled up with handsome works, of well-known
    names,
Selected from the literature of earth—
Where serious thinking teemed, and also mirth.
Novels from Fielding down to Hawthorne's son.
Cervantes, Swift and Dickens, furnished fun.
Essays from Bacon down to bold Carlyle's;
Biography from Plutarch down to Smiles's;
Tales from Boccaccio's time down to Bret Harte.
Philosophy mankind was loth to part,
Aristotle's the great, now faring ill;
And Combe and Spencer, Darwin, Huxley, Mill.
Music from Foster back to Bonnie Doon;
Histories from Herodotus to Hume.
Theology from Paul to Frothingham;
Critiques from Addison, Haslett and Lamb.
Wisdom from goodly minds of Field and Town—
Ike Walton, Fuller and Sir Thomas Browne.
    Assembled in this room our travelers
Felt as contented as do birds in firs
When outside storms are howling, hurting not,
Nor mar their pleasures in a sheltered spot.
Within this room all quickly felt at ease,
And each one tried the other one to please.
Some looked around upon the pictured wall;
Some said the weather was like days in fall.
While others talked and argued, many read,
Or joked about what such a one had said.

Some talked about the healthfulness and bloom
Which seemed to be about the sitting-room;
And, as they soon may be beyond our reach,
We'll try and take some items down of each.
    The Professor, rather an oddish man,
Had skin like parchment that was dipped in tan.
His eyes were small and black—back in his head—
And played accompaniment to what he said.
His education was more full than fair,
And never caused him trouble anywhere,
For egotistic was he, and quite thin,
And very easy could one flatter him.
His title where attained we do not know;
Report was he had traveled with a show.
What gave him most of pleasure, 'twas his tune,
Was his ascension once in a balloon.
He dressed himself not in the latest style,
In garments which might make some triflers smile;
And, though stiff of limb, he loved colors gay—
Cleanly and pleasing was his whole array.
His faults were many, but a kindly heart
Took from them what we'd call their selfish part,
And he was valued for a funny vein
That emanated from his curious brain.
O'er his dark face there never spoke or shone
A smile of mirthfulness more than if stone.
He was all solemnness unto himself,
Unto the world he was a comic elf;
Nature in making him had a good laugh,
So he kept sober in his own behalf.
    The Soldier had been out upon the plains
Afighting the Indians, without much gains.
He now was on a furlough, far from harm,
Nursing an old wound in his once strong arm.

In the Rebellion, where the thousands died,
He had been fighting on the stronger side
Gaining much honor for his bravery
In the great fight that settled slavery.
He was a captain now, could wear the bars,
Hoping no doubt they'd shortly change to stars.
His figure was not built on a tall plan;
He was a bantam-rooster of a man;
But game withal, and ever carried high
A head whose raven curls had ne'er known dye.
He was unmarried still, but sought a wife;
Had been a fortune hunter all his life.
Had many asked since first his task begun,
But others proved more fortunate and won.
None but the brave deserve the fair, is said;
Yet, somehow, they took cowards in his stead.
Hope never leaves a soldier, so he thought
That time would bring the jewel that he sought.
He was no braggart, but his toss of head
Gave that impression more than all he said;
For modesty of words and haughty mien,
Though seemingly absurd, are often seen.
    The Mechanic, his hair was nearly gray,
Hard work or thinking made it look that way.
He still was young in years, not thirty-five,
With all his passions thoroughly alive.
He had in youth made up his vigorous mind
To get as rich as any of his kind—
Succeeding even much beyond his aim,
Though doing nothing tarnishing his fame.
He had, in bringing the result about,
Acted as of rest he could do without,
When getting wealthy by his contracts large—
Raising the splendid structures in his charge.

His personal appearance only ran
Within the usual average type of man.
His special feature was a massive mouth,
The lines of which curved more toward north than
      south,
And underneath it a great ponderous chin
Which well might bless or curse a child of sin.
His manners were polite with easiness,
And he had sympathy for real distress.
Was owner of a monster tenement;
Nor worthy ones would he put out for rent
When winter made the earnings of the poor
Too small to keep e'en hunger from the door.
He was a man quite careful of his deeds,
Living as sumptuous as his nature's needs,
In the high roads of literature and art
He seldom tried to enter and take part.
He was a man exemplifying high
The worth of the activity of " Try;"
Showing that will and pluck, with active mind,
Can always leave the opposite behind.
    The Minister was tall, and prim, and spare;
His clothes fitting exactly, and his hair
Was neither black nor white,but simply gray—
With yellow tinge alike unto bad hay.
His voice was soothing as might be a saint;
His eloquence had thrice made women faint.
Afflicted was he with a nose so red
That scoffers hinted such a thing was fed
With deep potations, but the thought was
    false.
A little wine he drank, with Rochelle salts,
This e'en to please the doctor of his wife,
Who reasoned that it might prolong his life.

He now was bound for the clear mountain lakes,
Not for rose-fever, but to cure the shakes.
His parsonage was built where land was low,
And badly drained, and brought him much of woe.
His people were not radical nor queer,
But gave him two month's respite every year.
His family however were near home,
Nor could they well afford so far to roam,
For use a paltry income as you can,
Most of its luxuries do go to man.
He was a man of kindness, peace on earth,
Without pretense to frown on gentle mirth;
One of those good square souls we sometimes see
Upon life's journey, full of charity.
  The Doctor was a man with silvery hair;
Brought up a shoemaker, he did declare.
His coronal of head of hair was void.
By too much thinking was the brain employed;
Or, as he said, the cause of it was that
When he was young he wore a tight silk hat.
He had a well shaped head, a pleasant face,
Where rippling sunshine left full many a trace.
He often failed when men he tried to cure;
So that some persons thought his skill was poor;
But strange it were sick women made he well,
Unless too aged for his healing spell.
And as for children, one he never lost,
Which saved to parents many a funeral cost.
The needy helped he with an open hand,
And famished looks were more than he could stand.
He now was traveling to restore his health,
Taking no drugs to bring him back that wealth.
Himself he taught, believed in good fresh air;
Let them take drugs who would, he did not care.

He was of age when men do idly boast,
And loved his cup of tea and buttered toast.
  The Lawyer was a man with dusky hair
Which stood erect above a forehead fair
Holding more knowledge than the average man;
With much ability to think and plan.
The sciences of sense he read much in,
But with Theology he was less kin.
Facts were his fancy, logic was his wit,
Judgment with conscience did co-equal sit.
His hand was seldom open to the poor,
Though he thought hard all poverty to cure,
For theoretically he was kind,
However much his practice was behind.
His brain had brought him much of store and
        wealth;
Its overworking left him wretched health.
A stomach, that for years he'd hardly own,
Now claimed attention, causing many a moan.
His clients' thoughts of him were much com-
        plex,
As never tried he them to please or vex,
Yet had a winsome kindness in the way
He did salute whoe'er he met each day.
It may be nobler beings lived than he,
But honest was he and good company.
  The Gambler was a man of quiet grace,
Blessed with a thoughtful and an earnest face.
A broken nose gave it a quaintly trim,
Which was a source of much regret to him.
Some years agone, when in a gambling fray,
He got so marred, expecting better pay.
His pockets were not always outward bent,
As money quickly got is quickly spent.

Now by what pleased him to call Fortune's wheel,
He had the cash for tour and luscious meal.
A simple conscience did within him lurk,
Which gave him much respect for nature's work,
So in the woods he'd ne'er consent to play—
They seemed to make him think that he should
       pray;
However, when he sought the gaudy town,
Then his good resolutions tumbled down.
He would not hoard, in this he was to blame,
Lacking no doubt some useful part of brain.
When on the top right royally he fared,
And his successes with the world he shared.
He was what cynics might expect to see
As representing this frail century.
A mind ideal, but opposed to law,
Perverted, that its fancy was a flaw;
Reason a painted anchor, made of wood,
Useless but ornamental—little good.
  The Broker was a man with shaven face,
Who often frequented the barber's place,
To make him look far younger than his years,
And more respected by his elder peers.
His spine in childhood had been nearly broke;
Of his appearance he would brook no joke.
He was a dandy, wore the best of clothes;
Was very careful of his shoes and hose.
An honored member of the Stock Exchange,
While the Gold Board was once within his
       range.
He and a brother made up a strong firm
That no mad panic ever had made squirm.
Our Broker was a rich man's eldest born,
Unmarried still, but not at all forlorn.

He was a man that understood the town,
And never to his business played the clown.
Men of less wealth than he were farther seeing,
But few, if any, were more persevering.
Take him at his own trade he's hard to beat;
At other things his equal's in each street.
Earth is to him a land of milk and honey,
And what he well can use he gets for money.
Should time, by trials, ever make him mellow,
Doubtless he'll make a refined, jolly fellow.

The Merchant was a man of rustic sense,
Of which he prided more than competence.
He was indifferent to much men love—
E'en boasted that he never wore a glove.
His clothes were of the choicest fabric, while
The cut of them was in a long past style.
Some forty years ago 'twas doubtless wise,
Though now it gave the public a surprise;
For oddness will attract the crowd this way,
Or if too modest or, extremely gay.
He lived a temperate life, liked native wheat,
Unbolted, and in diet kept from meat.
He believed water good for man and beast,
While a warm bath he liked more than a feast.
Some shooting pains, and tremors, were his ills,
For which he took no nostrums, wines or pills.
Friction, he thought, was all that was required,
With mountain air, which he so much admired.
He was quite rough in many ways to see,
Yet had a sort of bearish courtesy.
His face once seen could not be soon forgot—
Fitting to deck a debauchee or sot.
Ah, who could tell how many a battle he
Had fought to keep his life in purity?

And such a face, and yet a blameless life,
Teach struggling ones to hope mid passion's strife.
He was a man now growing rather old,
Who might be quickly taken off with cold;
And apoplexy lurked within his blood—
All this unto his mind seemed understood—
Yet never sighed he when the day was done,
Nor frowned in anger at the harmless fun.

The Driver was a man of thought and note,
Who through all seasons wore an overcoat.
His form was tall, bizarre and somewhat grand;
He could all weathers with much ease withstand.
He loved great nature, whether warm or cold,
And her extremes had doubtless made him bold.
He knew the regular tourists very well,
And the attractive parts of mount and dell.
He knew the streams where played the speckled
      trout;
He knew the time each night the moon was out.
He had laid by enough of wealth and store
So he might now enjoy, nor labor more,
But often, through the year, his friends would seek
To bring him from retirement, many a week,
And they could do it for his constant prayer
Was to have leisure for his friends to care.
He'd take them through the glorious mountain
      woods,
Through sublime gorges, by the lakes and floods,
To wayside inns, where he was almost host,
And every keeper made of him the boast.
He had some failings, yet his virtues shone
So much above them that they seemed alone—
Giving the blush to slander, and the hate
Of them who'd try to slur a nature great.

He worshipped at the shrine of many a maid,
But ne'er proposed, of them he was afraid.
He worshipped at a distance, foolish man,
Thinking the fair were angels under ban.
The sphere he filled in life it was not high,
Though his ideals reached up to the sky.
Take him for all, or half, he was a man
Who did his best, do better him who can.
   The Poet was a vagabondish one,
Who might have lived in ages that are gone.
A sort of dreamer, with some common sense—
More brains in head, than e'er he made pre-
      tense.
His coal-black hair he always wore in curls,
So as to draw the admiring glance of girls.
His rhyming work ne'er brought him many
      dollars;
Only about enough for hats and collars;
But a rich uncle, who was of him vain,
Helped him to that which often proved his bane.
In some respects he was a gallant man,
In others he seemed under nature's ban;
Or, else he failed to use what she bestowed,
And stead of trying with the current flowed.
Take him at his full worth he had good days
That made the world look brighter by his lays.
He loved the woods, he loved all nature's looks,
The midnight stars, the oceans, and the brooks.
He had the soarings of the vivid mind
That flies past reason, leaving it behind,
And skips the slower methods of the soul,
That go along with gait like to the mole,
And, I've to chronicle, to make it clear,
That when in town he liked his Lager Beer.

With all his faults his heart was in the right,
And for the weak and downcast he would fight.
  The budding Woman was a handsome elf—
Fully competent to look after self.
Her nose was of the Roman type, but small;
The convex bridge seeming to have a fall
Since the war times when Cæsar crossed the
    stream,
In the aggression of a warrior's scheme.
She was an author, who might like to vote;
Had lectured thrice, and rambling sketches
    wrote;
Besides a novel and a dress satire,
And a long rhyme not wanting strength or fire.
She had a happy look, a lovely face—
Fitting to beautify and bless her race.
She was yet single, somehow she tarried,
Yet had no great objection to get married.
Her robes were modest ones, but rich and plain,
Though cut not far off from the fashion's reign,
And from her ears two golden balls hung low;
Her wavy hair tied in a ribbon bow.
She was a being that the world might own,
And never bring to it a blush or groan.
Careless, but elegant; refined and sweet;
Natural, but cultured; affable and neat.
This woman had some wit, as one may guess,
And full of airy, bright suggestiveness.
So, seeing Chaucer, laying there so hoary,
Proposed that all the guests should tell a story;
Or, if the fancy acted strange or wrong,
To give a reading be it short or long.
"Agreed, agreed," cried they in haste to please;
For her sweet sake they'd fall upon their knees.

Her girlish beauty had the power to bend,
And make the roughest mortal a good friend.
So 'twas agreed each one should do his best
To tell a tale, to entertain the rest;
Or, if imagination needed weeding,
From some stray volume present give a reading.
As the result of compact, short and clear,
The readings which they gave do here appear.

THE POET.

FEW can know well the mind of him who sees
   The unwritten Scripture in the works of God;
Whose sight can reach far out into void space
And see the secrets hidden in the stars,
And read the records of the human heart,
Beating the same beat through a million years.

He, the true poet, is a mystery
Unto himself as to the common crowd,
He lives his life not in the realm of sense,
But in the realm of soul; he gives his hours
Freely to work that will in time uplift
Out of the sloughs of doubt the growing man.

Unto the crowd he seems to dwell alone;
But who would deem him lonesome when he
    hath
Bright forms around him, coming ever, going—

Heroes and sages, women divinely fair—
All those called by his brain forth from the
    depths,
The saints and saviors, and the kings and queens ?

All houseless may he seem unto the crowd;
And yet within his mind a palace stands,
Filled with the richest furniture and gems,
And marbles pure from unknown fairy lands,
And carpets like fair lawns in May or June,
And ceilings with the frescoes of the skies.

The crowd may deem him lacking harp and reed;
And yet the music of the universe
He hears, and voices filled with melody
From far-off planets come to cheer his soul,
And symphonies borne to him, on the wind,
From islands by whose shores the mermaids sing.

Unto the crowd, he seldom travels far;
And yet all nature comes before his eyes.
He sees the battle in the distant field;
He sees the mighty storm, where ships go down;
He sees the dreary mountains of the moon;
He sees the spread of knowledge through the
    world.

He hath nor God nor heaven, unto the crowd,
And yet his thoughts flow upward straight to Him,
The Mind that rules the system of the spheres,
That works eternally but for the best;
And his soul holds communion with the lost
Who dwell somewhere beyond the mortal stars.

THE CHOIR IN THE SKY.

THERE'S a choir in the sky
   Once earth's poets were they,
Who e'en bless earth to-day—
Watching singers pass by
   From our sphere on the way
To their new homes on high,
   To a welcome convey,
And the heavens glorify.

Once on hearing them sing—
   Was I trance-like? I found
   They were gathering around,
Emerson's soul had taken wing,
   Through my heart pleasure bound.
And their harps had a ring
   Of great beauty—a sound
To the mind comfort bring.

More majestic and sweet
   Than the songs often sung
   In our mundane rasp tongue,
Seemed to me their rare treat.
   Their true viols seemed strung
In an Orphean feat;
   While their vocal tones rung
In resonance replete.

Though possessed of a lyre
　That would nourish the soul,
　Each day nearing the goal—
Mind toward sky—I'd aspire
　To a name on the scroll
Of that weird poet-choir;
　Or would sing mirth and dole
To their welcome inspire.

THE LEGEND OF LOVE.

THE present age has legends, too,
　And rich as long ago,
With skies as full of light and blue,
　And human hearts aglow
With love, as when Boccaccio wrote
　Those quaint immortal scenes,
Where through his changing fancies float
　A bevy of fair queens.

I see the walls of memory's dome
　With pictures covered o'er;
I see thereon a mass of foam,
　A wreck, and rock-bound shore.
The past, once fair, now dim and pale,
　Looks shuddering in my face;
The glorious goals, once in my hail,
　Now fly from my embrace.

I see the duties that I gave
  Unto the winds, flash by;
I see them mount on pleasure's wave,
  And move a-lee and die.
The burdens that I cast away
  Come back with greater weight;
I watch, but see no morning gray
  Dawn o'er the hills of fate.

But comfort greets me even there,
  And one on whom I gaze
Is lovely as the sylphs of air
  That tread the twilight haze;
It is my gracious first, first love,
  Her whom I loved in youth,
When on the tree of life above
  Still bloomed the flowers of truth.

O, she was bright as heavenly light;
  The moon through ether hurled
Ne'er looked down on a rarer sight
  Of beauty in this world!
The morning sun that gilds the spire,
  And glints o'er hill and dell,
Ne'er threw his brilliant gorgeous fire
  Upon a fairer belle.

What rapture laughed about my heart
  When first I saw that girl;
With what a thrilling, throbbing start,
  My brain was in a whirl!
The life of those sweet moments pen
  Could ne'er express in rhyme;
The thoughts of love, that ruled me then,
  No fairy bells could chime!

I more than loved that charming one;
   I loved her nights and days;
I loved her when the sun came on
   Majestic with his rays;
I loved her when his twilights paled,
   And gloomed above the lake,
While in the west the crescent sailed
   With Hesper in her wake.

I worshipped her through happy hours,
   And often in my dreams
She moved before my inner powers
   In Paradisal gleams.
I saw her with the angels pure,
   In supermundane bliss;
I saw her while my soul secure
   Gave her devotion's kiss!

Ah, what if life's a mystery,
   And full of griefs and sighs,
If I behold, this side death's sea,
   An angel with mine eyes?
And what if death must be my friend
   Passing the pearly bars,
If I may meet where two worlds blend,
   My love beyond the stars?

She is the herald of the sphere
   Seen by prophetic sight,
A splendid vision sent us here
   To rid the earth of night.
All doubts and fears and all their brood
   My heart repels since I
Have had this vision of the Good,
   And seen the By and By,

AN INCIDENT IN THE SERVIAN ARMY.

HOW the General's heart-blood leaped and run
　　As a letter from home brought the news
That his wife was well and his new-born son;
　　All his home in his mind he reviews,
And a gleam of a tear comes to his eyes,
　　A gleam more of pleasure than pain;
His wife and his babes are as Paradise;
　　He'd deem himself there if home again.

A soldier now, a prisoner bound,
　　Before him sullenly is brought;
Minus two fingers has been found:
　　Done that he'd be discharged, 'twas thought.
Denied however that the deed
　　Was by himself or a coward's brand;
A comrade helped him in his need;
　　But he'd not name him by command.

"Art not ashamed," the General asked,
　　" Thus dastardly to hurt thy hand,
Our army in its work sore tasked,
　　The Turks upon our Fatherland?"
"Dear General, pardon," he replied,
　　" I've fought the Turks, ne'er shirked before,
And bravely charged where thousands died,
　　But I'd see wife and babes once more."

" Indeed," scornfully returned the chief,
  "Thy leave of absence I'll make long;
So say thy prayers, and make them brief,
  Prepare to die for this great wrong."
A soldier guard was here drawn out
  Before the prisoner, under ban,
Who crossed himself, stood grave and stout,
  For not a coward was this man.

Forgetting something he went o'er
  And placed within the General's hand
Some money pieces, three or four;
  He said, "My all—I own no land,
Let them be given to my wife
  When of my wretched death she hears."
"Go," said the General, "take thy life
  To her," his eyes brimmed round with tears.

THE FIRST BUTTERFLY.

BRIGHT flutterer, with golden name,
    Freckled from gentle dun to flame.
How hast thou dared to venture out
Ere the buds begin to sprout?

When underneath the sheltering bower,
Arbutus hath not shown her flower,
Creeping from the modest moss,
With her brilliant leaves of gloss:

When as yet within the brook,
Leaves lie pressed as in a book,
Held within the Ice King's arms
Clasped about their frozen charms;

Why wert thou not wise to wait
Till King Frost should abdicate?
Till the bluebirds pipe in tune,
Till the May looks on toward June,
Till the dandelion's yellow
Lends the lawn a radiance mellow?

These few hours of sunshine warm
May prelude a fatal storm,
Bringing frost or bringing snow;
Where, then, frail one, wilt thou go?
Robin's forty times as strong,
Yet we do not hear his song.

WITHIN THE GATES.

IN waking dreams, that bring us gleams
   Of what has been and what will be
We harbor Thought that kindly seems
   To ope the gates of destiny;
We see its light bring dawn and rise,
Flooding the vistas of our skies,
   And whether qualified or not
The mind gives welcome to the guest,
   And would unfold it, that forgot
It might not be till man does rest.

Back, back, until the bygone hours
   Are with us like the present now;
On, on, and forward to the powers
   Yet coming slowly to endow
The unborn cycles, till at last
Man on the earth's but of the past—
   When Desolation working well,
With Chaos, has the victory won;
   Hurling through space the orbs that fell
Toward the abysses of the sun.

Ah! man thought once he could survive
   The ruthless forces which he knew
Were coming, valiantly alive,
   Which well might him and his subdue.
Ah! robust one—upon the brink
Of death he was impelled to think

That, notwithstanding changes dire,
The wisdom of his intellect
   Could be a match for cold or fire,
Or seeming infinite neglect.

The moon, though ages so admired,
   Earth's satellite, or sister sphere,
Now changed was to twin-circles fired
   Surrounding it.   They did appear
Like Saturn's rings ere they combined
And with their planet forces joined,
   When Titan changes formed them life
And glorious spheres from galaxies,
   With beauty and enchantment rife,
To roam the future stellar seas.

Earth had become like lifeless stone,
   Man having vanished from its crest;
While plans and hopes, that he alone
   Engaged and cherished, were at rest.
Yet there were globes that still had life
Upon their surface, joy and strife,
   Where God was still the paradox
Of understood and mystery;
   The key creation's door unlocks,
And vague opaque eternity.

REST IN INFERNO.

TO Michael the Archangel came the mandate,
    well
To guide St. Paul through Heaven and then
    through Hell;
They visited the Heavens and saw therein
Felicity and beauty with no stain of sin;
Each spirit there symmetrical and wise;
Pure heavenly joyousness to all ears and eyes;
St. Paul was happy, and aloud he cried:
"For this He lived, was crucified and died,
And the result is ample for the deed
Of Him by Whom from Death mankind was
    freed."

The Archangel Michael with the great St. Paul
Went down into the Hells, and saw them all.
But the Apostle, at the fearful mark
Evil had made, and with it all the dark
Distress of soul, and bodily agony,
Was shocked with sympathy, as he well might
    be,
And to his escort earnestly he cried:
"Have they no respite here?" to which replied
The Archangel: "No Sabbath know they here,
But evermore these scenes of woe and fear."

Then to the Master, prayerfully Paul said;
"Lord, I have seen the wicked, doubly dead,

My heart, dear Lord, is burdened by their fate.
Though their transgressions from Thy laws are
    great,
Grant Thou a day of rest to these forlorn
In memory of Thy resurrection morn!''
And ever since, the wise are wont to say,
The wicked rest in Hell each Sabbath Day.

ON THE FRONT PLATFORM.

IT rained, and when I got aboard
    That car, the lowering weather
Made every one feel dull and cross.
    We were alone together,
The driver and myself; I passed
    My nickel through the door; his throat
Was in a muffler, and he looked
    Betwixt a Southwold and a shote.

He smiled good-naturedly, then took
    From out his ample waterproof
An orange; 'twas a splendid sphere—
    He held it from his mouth aloof—
'' My teeth are watering all day long
    To eat this juicy fruit,'' he said;
'' I got it on my early trip—
    On such food are the favored fed.''

" Why not indulge and eat?" I said;
  " This self-denial's hardly right."
" Nay," said he; "you should see my boy;
    He is, indeed, a comely sight.
  Of two years old he lacks a month.
    I've a swing off, an hour, at seven;
  I eat my supper at my home,
    And there I get a slice of heaven.

" When I get home, though somewhat tired,
    I try to be myself a while,
  And when I toss this to my boy,
    You'll see that merry youngster smile.
  I'll think no more of the freezing weather,
    The lagging hours, the little pay,
  The comforts of the millionaires—
    You're getting off—well, friend, good day!"

A MAN SHOULD BE JUDGED AS
A MAN.

MEN there are that lay claim for approval
    On the feeling, that is merely of earth,
Thinking they have the right in religion,
    And that some favorite land gave them birth,
Who look down with bad eyes and derision
    On who come from a different place.
And who may differ with them as to Heaven,
    And to Deity, destiny, race.
No, no; men should not be so vain;
    Make your birthplace, man, if you can!
Religion's oft shaped by the brain—
    A man should be judged as a man.

Was in England the place he saw morning?
    Was it Ireland that first met his sight?
Was in Scotland the hills of his childhood?
    Was it Wales where he first saw the light?
Is it Russia the nation that claims him?
    Or in Germany first breathed he air?
Or in France, Spain, Holland or Sweden—
    Or America, Asia, or where?
Fy, fy; love of country is just—
    But each man has rights in this plan;
Slaves strut them on mountains of dust—
    A man should be judged as a man.

Is he noble, and to his word steadfast?
  Does he pay to the workers what's right?
Or labors he for they who employ him,
  In true friendship, with vim and delight?
Has he charity for earth's poor weak ones?
  Does he worship a greater than pelf?
Does he grant all the rights to another
  That he claims and demands for himself?
Yes, yes; there is good in all this;
  Such doings are on a high plan;
In poverty's hell or in bliss
  A man should be judged as a man.

THE WOMAN IN CAMP—1854.

THE sight of a woman was rare in those days;
  So Deep Cañon Camp was set in a blaze
When the rumor was started, and sent by each
    door—
A woman had got there the evening before.

The excitement spread wide, away on the breeze
Rose racket and cheers, to where the red trees
Shadowed the gulches, for the thoughts of each man
Were intent on the woman, not on pick, nor on pan.

Ah, never a miner within all the camp
But out toward the cabin which held her would
    tramp;
Eager the gathering, they envied, ah yes,
The fellow who caught but a glimpse of her dress.

The husband, nonchalent, came to the crowd,
And as he appeared Jim Blonde spoke aloud:
"Fetch her out here, Lord bless her, she's a
    surprise;
We hunger to see her; its good for weak eyes."

"My wife she is sick, and I, too, feel bad,
Been robbed by the Indians, lost all that we had."
But Jim Blonde, the speaker, said in reply,
"Bring out the woman, we won't let her die."

She came to the front, her face in a smile
That went to the heart of each miner meanwhile;
And welcomes were given, some rough, and all
    strong,
Mid waving of hats, and cheers loud and long.

Three thousand, in gold, was raised there and then
Given, with pleasure, by rough-bearded men;
Well, the sun will melt ice, and woman can make
The heart of a Midas to melt for her sake.

MY OLD CANTEEN.

I BRING you out, my old canteen,
    Near twenty years have passed between
The time I saw you last, old friend.
I love to think that at my end
You may be present, generous one,

That gave until your all was gone,
And filled again your good quart pouch
For march, for battle, for the couch.
Of all the friends I've known or seen,
None was your better, old canteen.

Dost recollect, when we held the bridge,
When Hayniman crept o'er the ridge,
Crushed by a sword blow in the head?
How kind you were, for when he said
That he was thirsty, all you had
You gave in welcome, and were glad
That you could ease his thirst.   We sighed
At his misfortune.   Well, he died.
Much of the war's grief have we seen,
You and myself, my old canteen.

I well know when I saw you first;
I had not then been much athirst;
You were respectable looking then.
I know I was much younger when
I grasped you in my hand, and slung
You o'er my shoulder; we were young.
Moth eaten now's your dusty coat,
And partly rusty is your throat;
But no new one shall come between
Our old-time love, my good canteen.

You know the men who kissed your lips,
Some died in battle; some in ships
Have ventured far from port; and some
Still wear the uniform, hear the drum.
Some turned from the good drink you gave—
One fills I know a drunkard's grave.

Some in the fight for daily bread
Are quite successful; some are dead.
Few better men were ever seen
Than shared your love, my old canteen.

THE TWO BLOSSOMS.

TWO blossoms grew upon one tree,
  And both of them were dear to me.

I watched them through their budding time,
And through their beauteous early prime.

A torrid tempest came one day,
And deadly ruin marked its way.

Alas! it struck the weaker one,
And soon its bloom and life were gone.

Under the burning breath it fell,
'Mid tears of those who loved it well.

The other still stands brave and strong,
At morn, at noon, at vesper song.

To it the fatal fever bane
Was only nutriment and gain.

It grows so hale, so sweet, so fair,
Amid God's all-embracing air,

Its life at each and every stage
Adding more beauty to the age.

Oh, soul of man! go search and see
If thou canst question Diety.

I bring two blossoms to that shrine,
Two of the dearest ones of mine.

O Father Mind! can we not clasp
Thy answer in our mental grasp?

When both have done with this blue dome
And entered to Thy higher home,

Shalt Thou not love the weaker flower
As much as that which lived its hour?

Shalt Thou not make the weak one grow
And gain all that is missed below;

While through the epochs of all time
We hail Thy equal love sublime?

SORREL.

MUSING to-night on former years,
    The war unto my eyes appears,
And mid it memories—hopes and fears—
    My mind goes back to Sorrel.

That faithful war steed's now no more,
That me through dangers safely bore,
Yea, through the raids and battles' roar;
    For dauntless was good Sorrel.

When the war ended, his fine head
He laid upon earth's chilly bed,
And soon he slumbered with the dead;
   And so breath left poor Sorrel.

Why did he so ignobly die?
He that so oft heard bullets fly,
While shells burst through the sulphurous sky;
   Ay, why did they spare Sorrel?

Stout horse! he bore me o'er the soil
On many a weary march of toil,
While the hot sun made the blood boil;
   But through it all went Sorrel.

He oft has chased guerrilla bands
O'er ditches wide and swampy lands,
And helped to fetter traitors' hands;
   For swift was my good Sorrel.

He, too, has charged with flying feet,
And followed up the dire retreat,
Where the rebels got so badly beat;
   Ay, you were there, brave Sorrel!

Poor horse! you're now at peace. The strife
Of man no more effects your life,
That with all nobleness was rife;
   And so good night, brave Sorrel!

AT THE GATE.

ALONE, and by the garden gate she stands,
 Watching the tender twilight as it lends
To our good earth a dreamy atmosphere,
That in these calmly sweet September days
Enters the soul like echoes of old hymns,
Which we have heard in twilights of the past,
Giving contentment with this world of ours.

Her forehead fair is fanned by gentle gales;
Her yellow hair is waving in their waves;
And her fair person, in the mellow air,
Looks like a denizen of Paradise
Just dropped to earth to see it go asleep,
With all its millions, in the arms of Night.

She has no lover yet, but in her mind
There has grown up a vague, uncertain dream
Of what perchance her other part may be;
And, like a lonely bird in early spring,
Her gentle breast is fluttering for its mate.

So in her musing, at this twilight hour,
While star by star comes out into the night,
And planets seem not a day's journey off,
She's wishing that the world may grant to her
Some one to fill the niche within her heart,
That has been vacant, but not known before—
Some sweet and ardent nature that will love
Her for herself through all the coming years.

AFTER THE MASQUERADE.

A YOUTH in London at a masquerade
All dressed up as a prince, his part well
played,
Greatly enjoyed the dance
With a princess of France,
A witch from the bizarre times
Of castles and romance rhymes.

So overjoyed was he
At the rainbowed royalty
Which his dress bestowed
In its shimmering load,
His mind went astray,
In some wayward way,
And he really believed
He was Wales himself,
With the power and pelf :
He was so deceived.

Next morn, ere the hour of nine by the clock,
At the palace door he tried to knock,
Arrayed for the pageantry,
And all feathered and free,
Claiming entrance there
As the rightful heir
Born the crown to wear.

Poor head! turned strange through the power
And the charm of a gala hour;
Arrested, put past lock and key!
All for his tinselled pedigree.

Let us have pity for this son of earth!
Shall we say, Alas, for his simple birth?
Ay, the birth of one is the birth of all!
The Savior was born in an humble stall,
And what czar or prince or chief is he
Who can claim a nobler pedigree?

THE MAN IN THE MOON.

WHEN the silvery orb of the night is near full,
    You may see on its face, late or soon,
That effigy vague known to children and scalds
    As the Man in the Moon.

This man in the moon sits aloft in a tree,
    And one of his functions up there
Is to wait on the mythical Queen of the Night,
    A woman that's fair.

This woman's a goddess with many a name,
    But Cynthia's the one I admire;
She reigns through the hours after the sun
    Has put out his fire.

The man in the moon watches sharp to be sure
    When the shepherd, her lover's, asleep,
Endymion by name, who pastures his flock
    Where Latmos is steep.

Fair Cynthia gently comes down when he sleeps
    To kiss him most lovingly there;
And who wouldn't wish such a shepherd to be,
    To be kissed by the fair?

Yet they who are wiser than old-time romance,
  Dare tell us the man and the tree,
When viewed through the telescope vanish from
      sight,
  And are dead as can be.

But Science, avaunt! in the man and the tree,
  And Cynthia, loving and bright,
We firmly believe, though not ours is her kiss
  In the moonshine to-night!

A WAIL FOR WALT WHITMAN.

GONE over the border land to the haven of rest,
      tired voyager !
Old mother earth is gracious, and she received thee
    with open arms.
She knows her children at sight, and loves and
    glorifies them,
And in her embrace she took thee to keep at her
    heart forever.

Who would not be such a poet, to be loved by such
    a mother?
Who would not be such a son, to feel such a
    mother's attractions?
Thou wert narrow as sin, yet broad as the uni-
    verse's pulse beats,
To sing that grime and shine, even as flower and
    gem were perfection.

A passionate heart hadst thou, with love for thyself
    and thy kindred,
Who were of the high and low, no special exclu-
    sion for any;
And if there were few tears shed on thy grave, in
    the Jersey clearing,
It may not be because worthier ones are lying un-
    wept and forgotten.

Another's not left with us now to show the full
    glory of freedom;
The flight from the classic and prim to the fresh-
    ness and grasses of nature;
The might of the ocean, the factories exalting and
    vengeful,
The great spirit of cities, and the audacity even of
    prairies!

CARDINAL MANNING'S PALTRY PURSE.

THIS august personage of ripened age,
    Through whose good hands vast fortunes
    passed for years,
Had fed the poor so bountifully well,
Had wiped the tears from off so many eyes,
That can we marvel at him, almost bare,
Or surprised or shocked at the trifle left
(A washwoman had a heavier purse)—
"A sixpence, shilling, sovereign and a half."

Ideals of the Master ruled his life,
And all his building was for Paradise,
While others hoarded gold and sought estate,
The plaudits of the world—the cheer, the fame.
More selfish he, yet higher, who saw earth
A footstool in the primary school of spheres—
A harbinger of joys ineffable—
An atom in the palace where God dwells.

He knew it!   'Mid the eyeless he had sight,
And where most others saw but barren wolds—
Fit sepulchres for dead to mold and rot—
He saw earth's flowers transfigured to the skies;
He saw the wheat growths of Eternity.

SONG OF THE UPLANDS.

O BETTER a glimpse of a star
   That may never be reached but be hoped for;
O better a grand life afar,
   That at least in the mind can be groped for,
      Than to have all the senses desire,
      And all that the passions require,
         But no more, but no more.

O better a faith that can cope
   With the doubts of the world and can quicken;
O better a life that has hope
   To illume it, though poverty stricken,
      Than to have all that riches can hire
      Or buy, so to feast and not tire,
         But no more, but no more.

O better a love that is blind,
   That can see in the loved one no badness;
O better a trust in one's kind,
   Spite of all of its folly and madness,
      Than to stand all alone mid earth's mire,
      Having food and raiment and fire,
         But no more, but no more.

MOUNTAINS AND FOOTHILLS.

DEVELOPED human nature is greater than
   nationality;
Nor can aught creed be large enough to take in
   infinite wisdom.
Men of high thought the world over are harmon-
   iously minded;
Worship the self-same God, or ideas of it material;
Honor Virtue and Truth, and their many attend-
   ants beautiful.
'Tis only the somewhat warped who harp on their
   creed or their nation;
As if the Beneficent showed prejudice toward
   temples and places!

AFTER—B. W. D.

IF we but knew what web and woof
  Time, all so passive, would work out,
    We would have taken a different part.
The past is closed.   It needs no proof
  To show I honored him; no doubt
    In these words of a sincere heart.

I loved him by what I learned of friends,
  But never saw his kindly face
    Until Death's pale lips had him kissed,
And now, remorseful, my soul sends
  This message, that would him embrace,
    Appreciating what I missed.

Worthy was he to claim as friend;
  Liberal enough for all mankind;
    High in the generous ways of life;
Accepting thought the world to mend.
  To gentle graces he inclined,
    Cherished his children, loved his wife.

I wished so much that we had met,
  Feeling his heart throb in hand clasp,
    In his companionship to be,
His robust heartiness to get;
  Of his life atmosphere to grasp
    A share, and eye to eye him see.

It may not be.   Yet I would weave
  This simple tribute o'er his grave
    In sorrow for his early fate,
While tenderly my heart does grieve
  For those he left behind, and crave
    A greeting for this offering late.

OUTSIDE THE NARROWS.

I GAZE towards the far-off sea,
    Nearly unknown it is to me;
Ships ride at anchor in its tide
Or swiftly o'er its waters glide;
Some are so far they lose all form,
Or look like snowflakes in a storm;
While others rise so clear and near,
They almost seem already here
In port secure from furious gales,
With sunshine on their folded sails.

Oh ships, upon the further sea,
Have you no news to give to me?
Have you not seen from your lookout—
Have you not hailed with welcome shout—
Them that I knew in other days,
That went beyond my mortal gaze?
Oh, are they safely sailing now,
With steadfast course and sturdy prow?
Or meet they storms by night and day
Mid rock-bound straits, far, far away?

Some, it is true, seem near to me,
Almost as on this earthly sea;
Bright forms serene in pure array,
That could not wholly pass away;
While some, like shadows, float through haze
More dimly than in other days.

God shield all those, whoe'er they be,
That move upon that further sea;
And keep them from the evil blast,
And bring them unto peace at last!

TAKEN AWAY.

WE'VE left what was our home for years,
  Though much we loved might keep us there;
Have tried to take away with us
  All that we valued, good and fair.

And though we've moved whate'er we owned,
  Of clothing, furniture or gain,
Much dearer to heart and memory
  About that house will long remain.

Would we could take away with us
  The little ones there entertained,
Who in a few but precious months
  The whole of our affections chained.

Sweet blooms, that Heaven on us bestowed,
  Yet kept their rootlets up on high;
No wonder that we could not keep
  Those flowers, whose garden is the sky!

WHAT THE SABRE SANG.

THE sabre hung in its long resting-place,
  The fading twilight making hard to trace
Its curve upon the wall; the South wind blew,
And past my house some running horses flew.
I in a dream, somehow have surely seemed
Where shod hoofs rang and sabres brightly
    gleamed—
Where the scabbard's jingle with the night winds
    mingle
Bearing along the sabre's song.

  " Mount was the word, and he and I
    O'er Southern roadways galloping fly.
    Some ruddy drops upon my blade
    Might make a tender heart afraid,
    But made for raid and daring fight,
    Such trifles give to me delight.
    Who cares if women pale—e'en fair?
    My master may—why should I care?

  " The cut which cleft that skull atwain
    Was parried well, but all in vain;
    My master's arm was lithe and hale,
    'Twould cleave a helmet made of mail.
    His parry did avail him not,
    Beneath the sod he was to rot;
    He parried for the head alone,
    His heart was pierced—he fell as stone.

" Twilight was o'er Burnt Tavern's marge
When the enemy made on us a charge;
'Twas hard to tell that they were foes
Until their rebel yell arose.
Their bravest rider I clove down,
Nor cared I for the night cloud's frown,
Nor timid moon that veiled her face—
I warmed within his red embrace.

" Long have I hung upon the wall,
Awaiting for my country's call.
Are there no wrongs for me to right?
Are men turned cowards—will not fight?
I'd like some sinewy arm to draw,
And show my blade without a flaw;
But women now and children reign—
When will the brave days come again?

" O for a pillow in a hand
That could each cut and thrust withstand!
The foemen drawn up for the fight,
Yells of defiance at the sight.
The horses with their nostrils large;
The order given for the charge;
The onset—where the foe are beat;
The scurry—where they're on retreat.

" I'd give a share I own of life
To be again amid the strife
Down in the Swamp, 'mid cypress trees,
To battle for the Refugees.
The long-haired Colonel sank beneath
The cut I gave—jumping my sheath—
Ah, then I was just full of pranks;
The dark-eyed women gave us thanks.

" What is within that makes me feel,
  Telling my ranking heart of steel
  That year and year yet I must hang
  Upon this wall with many a pang ?
  My master eyes me much at times,
  Thinking me food no doubt for rhymes:
  I would he knew that in my heart
  I'd have betimes a war to start.

" O bugler, blow, adown the South!
  Artillery battery, clear thy mouth!
  Infantry corps, turn out and mass!
  The enemy come through the pass.
  Now cavalry, behold their flank;
  It must be broken, rank on rank!
  Charge on! Let's cut them left and right,
  Their onslaught shiver in this fight! "

Still in its long accustomed place it hangs,
And if it had full consciousness, some pangs
Would doubtless thrill it, for fools have tried
The glory of the sabre to deride.
I in a dream, somehow, have surely seemed
Where shod hoofs rang and sabres brightly
      gleamed—
Where the scabbard's jingle with the night winds
      mingle,
Bearing along the sabre's song.

INTIMATIONS.

WHILE the soul is idly musing,
　　On thoughts not its own choosing,
Oft there come clear intimations,
Intuitions, inspirations,
Telling of a future life,
Far beyond this mortal strife ;
And to-night, as we are going
With the current gently flowing,
Come lovely sentiments of peace,
And the mind asks no release
From the blessing of their charm,
Holding us from every harm.

We drift along the sacred walls,
Where the ivy's verdure falls,
And we think upon the graves
Whose grassy brink the river laves,
While the night is all around,
And the stillness is profound,
Save the moving, active part
Of each palpitating heart,
As we float upon the stream,
In a sort of mystic dream.

But see, as we approach our home,
How the great cathedral dome,
With its lofty golden spire,
Wears a crown of seeming fire

In the fluctuating light
Gleaming from the north at night,
With its colors green and red,
Where the electric shafts are spread !

And hark ! across the quiet waves,
From the dim cathedral naves,
Come sweet voices, singing lays,
Quaint and sweet of other days,
When the Savior and the saint
Were on earth without a taint ;
How the wonders that they wrought
Were beyond all human thought ;
How their benisons abide,
And how He was crucified.

Now they move in happy staves—
These soft voices—o'er the waves !
Coming down from Jacob's stair,
Where glide the blessed angels fair,
Or God's children rest at night,
Ere they mount into His sight.

How calm, how sweet this singing !
  Surely from celestial lands,
  Over boundless golden sands,
Are the echoes winging !
They fall with soothing on the soul
  That has long with pains contended,
Presaging rest, as when the goal
  Is reached and travail ended ;
Where hope and faith do close in sight,
Beyond our thought, of pure detight.

May we see and hear this way
When shall come our closing day ;
When shall come the twilight hour ;
When grows weak our vital power ;
When we're nearly done with life—
With its sorrow and its strife ;
When our hearts are waxing old,
And even fears and hopes are cold,
In our darkness and distress,
Longing for God's tenderness.
In that hour, oh, let there come
A great, brilliant light from Home,
With rich love and blessing rife,
Ushering in the better life ;
Voices singing may we hear,
Hopeful pæans, calm and clear,
From the mansions we shall see,
Welcoming both you and me.

TANTALUS.

A KING of the past was Tantalus :
  The gods who held court on Olympus
Invited him once to their tables,
To dwell in their glory and sunshine.

He thought he now was their equal ;
And fired by brim tankards of nectar
His mind was disturbed and unbalanced.
Far better he ne'er had been lifted.

He worshipped his children and loved them ;
But mightier far his great passion,
His desire for the greatest gods' favor—
A child, his beloved one, he slaughtered.

The Furies were gathered, and drove him
Down deep in the hells for his rashness,
To stay till the dead should be quickened,
To suffer in hunger and torment.

And the gods still dwell on Olympus ;
They need not man's foolish performance ;
But he who seeks truth and acts justly,
May freely partake at their tables.

LONGING.

YOU are out with the planets to-night ;
 And my soul was filled full of despair
As you flooded with beauty my sight
 And vanished in thin upper air.

Will you stop with great Mercury and Mars
 If they happen along in your way ?
Will you pass to the outermost stars ?
 But wherever you go, do not stay.

I am mindful of all your charms,
 As I linger here rugged, and plain ;
For beauty supernal has arms
 That conquer and madden the brain.

So while you're afar in the skies,
   Let no cloud veil the marvelous gleams
Of the brow and bewildering eyes
   That flash inspiration through dreams.

The night slowly weakens ; and soon
   As the heavenly lights disappear,
May the daybreak restore the dear boon
 · Of knowing once more you are near !

Hasten dawn, thou fair drier of tears,
   Bear to earth her far-wandering feet ;
Each hour is more tedious than years,
   As I wait her bright footfall to greet.

Well, to love and adore fills my soul ;
   Naught can ever deprive me of this ;
And the thoughts that I would not control
   Sweeten grief with a fanciful bliss.

ROAMING THROUGH WOODS.

ROAMING through woods in serious mood,
   Hearing far waterfalls play,
I found, almost in solitude,
   A crystal spring one day.

   Unseen ere this it might have been,
      And yet it clearly gleamed,
   Meandering off in discipline,
      While sun rifts o'er it beamed.

And so a thought in some careless breast,
  Secret almost and sure,
Is found when God's rays on it rest,
  A crystal rivulet pure.

ABOVE CAUSALITY.

WHERE ride the inner guides to-night?
  A snowflake fell upon my hand,
Soft as a spirit's touch, and white,
  Brought back from the interior land
Unto a mother's sight.

I heard some strains of music when
  The moon sank o'er the wood,
And if they never come again
  Their meaning well I understood:
The singers once were men.

Wouldst follow up the stair of beams—
  Good stars have dropped it for our kind—
To mount above the land of dreams,
  Where reason permeates the mind,
Where all exists and nothing seems?

Ah! pity for the soul of him
  Who never hears the saintly song,
Nor sees the beings on the rim
  Of the great zone, where all belong
When life has reached the cherubim.

RECEIVED FROM A CHILD.

AS others were writing our little one
　　Said, "To papa she too would write;"
Making an effort, and when it was done
　　'Twas sent in an envelope white.

Ah ! what pleasure it gave to receive it,
　　For its circles my heart entwined ;
Though few words were therein to relieve it,
　　And its paper had not been lined.

'Twas a quaint and beautiful letter,
　　Brimmed full of young effort sincere ;
Where 's the father from youngster got better,
　　Or one to be treasured more dear?

For a talisman choice I will choose it,
　　And when shaken by passions wild
For my safety I 'll gladly peruse it,
　　This letter received from a child.

She informs me the folks at home love me,
　　That she wishes that I were home ; .
That she prays to the angels above me
　　To watch over me while I roam.

Though but part of the alphabet 's in it,
　　And to many it seems a scrawl—
They could never tell where to begin it—
　　Yet I can understand it all.

EN ROUTE TOWARD GETTYSBURG.

FROM Col. Aylett, who wore the gray,
  We get the facts we here array:
Lee's invaders were on their way.

Passing a Pennsylvania town,
Greencastle, a modest village brown,
Women look out with fear and frown.

One the Old Flag as an apron wore;
Waved it with pride as she stood by her door,
While the soldiers in gray marched past footsore.

Daring these men—brothers, alas!—
To touch the flag this handsome lass
Tries to annoy them as they pass.

Her pluck and loyalty have charms;
Pickett salutes her, no one harms,
And one marching regiment carries arms.

Many salute her with a sigh,
Thinking of home with moistened eye,
As on toward Gettysburg they hie.

Sarah Smith was the name that she bore
When Gettysburg shook with the battle's roar.
On Fame's fair page put her name to the fore!

LET WORKERS UNITE.

L ET workers unite!
    The brain and the hand
Be nerved for the fight
  Now shaped in this land.

The slave women stitch,
  The slave man's a boor;
The rich grow more rich,
  The poor grow more poor.

There's freedom for all,
  And knowledge and bread;
Who mindeth the call
  With both shall be fed.

There's help for each one—
  The ballot shall preach
When ignorance's gone—
  Ay, plenty for each.

Who huggeth his chains
  Is not for this fight;
Where manhood remains
  Let workers unite!

ON THE BRONX.

HOW gayly, on this day of June,
   The Bronx flows, bowered in green,
With trees and vines and birds in tune—
   A fresh and varied scene!
And in a shady nook there shakes
   A boat in trim attire;
Three maidens are within; it makes
   A picture to admire.

How charming are they all! lithe forms,
   Arrayed in dainty dresses;
Tranquil of mind, no selfish storms
   Could dwell beneath those tresses;
And they are gathering sprays of flowers
   From drooping branches, laden
With perfumed blooms, to cheer the hours,
   For youth is with each maiden.

One with an oar (so archly faced)
   The boat to bank keeps press'd in;
Another, with fine features graced,
   On damask cushion's resting,
Receiving boughs from one who'd wake
   Dead hearts to life—a vision
That could delight the poet Drake,
   Who thought this stream Elysian.

O Bronx! meandering toward the sea,
　Through shadow and through lightness,
Never before thou'st seemed to me
　So full of life and brightness
As at this time, 'mid birds and boat,
　With maidens gathering flowers;
Like elves of fairyland afloat,
　They bless the passing hours.

THE SONNETEER.

THE lazy poet is the sonneteer,
　Who in his twice-seven lines puts all he
　　knows
Of something, be it wood, or mead, or rose,
Or love, or hate—a wedding, or a bier.
　He has his pattern always to his eyes;
His thought can soar but in this narrow space,
And be it Niagara or a pretty face,
　The limit his expansion ever ties.
The rivulet, within its confined bed
　Of rock or clay, can seldom burst its banks;
　Its song, though flushed, can never leave the
　　ranks
Of small endeavors.　With its proudest head
　'Tis but a small thing to the epic roar
　Old ocean dashes o'er a mighty shore.

THE SPARROWS.

OUTSIDE my garret window there's a roof,
 And there the lively sparrows love to come,
These wintry days, eager to get a crumb.
Though feathered warm, in brown and gray, not
 proof
Are they 'gainst hunger. From a ledge aloof
 They flurry down, alert and frolicsome;
 And then, again, they're sober-eyed and glum,
Anxious that I should give for their behoof.
They are abused by some, I freely own;
 And when I gave food I have seen them flare
 Away a while, as if they had a fear
Of unexpected harm; but ne'er a stone
Would I throw at these gossips of the air,
 That this dull weather fills with chatty cheer.

THE BIRD OF HOPE.

GOING through the park I hear thy cheerful
 song,
 Sweet bird of hope, song sparrow. At thy
 leisure,
 Ere other birds of spring come with their
 treasure,
Ere robins clear, and blackbirds harsh and strong,
And bluebirds meek, in thickets yet do throng.

Advance guard of the spring, thy dainty meas-
ure,
Though wintry winds prevail, thou singest with
pleasure,
The coming bud and flower all in thy song.
Sing, little teacher, to encourage us
Whom the March winds are chilling to the core;
Who see no spring nor evidence of flowers.
Ah, could we doubtful days enliven thus,
As thou dost on yon leafless branch so hoar,
Our world would fuller be of happy hours!

THE WOOD THRUSH'S SONG.

OFT have I listened to thy song, sweet bird,
  Trying to learn it so that I might sing
It to myself long after in the fling
And turmoil of the city, but a word
  Or note I learn not; thine enraptured strain,
So filled with beauty, strength and cadences,
Has with it so much tree, and lawn, and breeze,
  And consonance, that all my task's in vain.
As difficult to learn it as the song
  Made by the streamlet down the mountain side,
  Rising and lowering in a rhythmic slide,
Tinged by the zephyrs which the sounds prolong;
  But, like to it, it lingers when away,
  Within the mind, and haunts us many a day.

THE CATBIRD'S SONG.

"MA-YAA, ma-yaa," I hear the catbird crying
From out the thicket during day's warm
hours,
When partly resting his melodious powers,
Near cornfields waving in the zephyr's sighing.
But hear him in the morning hours rejoice,
In middle summer, when his young are growing!
Behold him then from yonder spruce spire throwing
His melody about in marvellous voice!
Alto, soprano, mezzo, high and low.
How frolicsome this homely fellow's notes
Break on the ear; and hear him when he quotes
From other birds, the rascal mimics so.
And he improves the others' trill or call,
For if he only tries, he beats them all.

AT THE ENCAMPMENT—W. T. H.

LIKE one appearing from the tomb, he came,
Rising my pulse-beats up to fever heat.
Long years 'twas as a dead man I did treat
His memory, and had sacred held his name,
And of his taking-off stern fate did blame;
But now he's in my vision, well, complete,
While I, all jocund, this new light can greet,
For life seems different—not so sad or tame—

A pleasant surprise 'tis to have him here.
  Deem thou, old friend, in future near to stay;
In many meetings we'll recall the old
Brave days gone by we fought with so much cheer
  That the Old Flag should conquer and have
      sway;
And stay Old Time our memories to unfold.

THE WELL BROUGHT OVER FROM HOLLAND.

FRONTING a bluff beside the Tappan Zee,
  Surrounded by green sward, bubbles a spring
Wherein the traveler, or the bird on wing,
May quench his thirst and quaff cool purity.
  Above, in Wolfert's Roost, once lived a King
Of Romance, he whose magic pen could bring
The Hudson Dutchman back for us to see,
The village vroow, or New Amsterdam grandee.
  He drank of your sweet waters, humble fount,
And made you famous; even children tell
The whimsical story of the imported well.
  You bubble merrily beneath Van Tassel's mount
And wayfarers still seek you, for your fame,
And for the love of Diedrich Knickerbocker's
    name.

A POET.

BRAIN fibred all for poesy, in this
 Slow humdrum age of science, work he
  would
Creating noble forms on which he could
Bestow a worth immortal. Granite, gneiss
And sandstone of the mind, all gave him bliss
 Inspired with soul of beauty, brotherhood;
 Then consciously, yet modestly, he stood
Enlarging right and joy that none need miss.
 Wrought by his glowing faculties, manifold,
Old ruins changed to homes for singing birds;
Sleepers of old romance new life began;
 The glories of the future were unrolled;
Fair women dead again spoke golden words,
And songs were born to cheer the perfect man.

THE ANGELUS.

TWO simple souls stopped by a peal of bells,
 Amid the evening shades softly descending,
As homeward from their daily labor wending,
They pause to pray while the sweet cadence swells:
 Two souls sincere, though lacking in book sense,
But knowing well the world invisible,
Listening, they hear more than the solemn knell
 Of sounding chimes to wake their reverence;

So worshipping and spiritual they appear.
　　Devout brain fibres of the very life
　　Are stimulated in the man and wife,
And they love God and feel the heavenly sphere;
　　They have no science raising mental mists
　　To blind the truth divine, that God exists.

WASHINGTON ROCK, NEW JERSEY.

HERE on this giant rock, backed by this wood,
　　He viewed the hostile red coats of the foe,
　　Led by Cornwallis on the plains below,
Noting their movements, while concealed he stood.
What a vast prospect was before his eyes,
　　Where now fair plains and pleasant towns
　　　　abound!
　　Yonder's the gray of Staten Island Sound,
And here the Raritan low winding lies.
New Brunswick's but a dozen jumps, you'd think,
　　O'er there the towers of Brooklyn Bridge so tall;
　　Yonder stands Liberty enlightening all;
And there's the gusty ridge of Navesink.
How varied are the scenes which spread below,
Where Washington once stood and watched the
　　　　foe.

A TAWNY HEAD FROM EGYPT.

WHERE rude curiosity cannot e'en debase
 It rests, this marvel from the antique land
Of pyramid and sphinx, and palm and sand,
(With tufts of hair, warm-bronze, within a case,)
An illustration of the dominant race
 That swayed the world for centuries, and that
  planned
 Archives of art and catacombs to stand
'Gainst all Time's efforts laboring to efface.
These sightless sockets once with love-light shone ;
 This brow command has given men among,
And with its intellect may have given tone
To governments—ay, even touched our own ;
 While lips, that might have greeted wife and young,
 Are now with brain that thought, with voice that
  sung.

PASSED OVER THE BRIDGE.—J. E. T.

WATCHING, through vigils long, the arch of
  light
 Spanning the bridge, uniting cities large,
 Who doubts his mind took note of all the charge
Approaching dissolution with its blight

Had put upon him? Through the long sad nights
He mused on life, death and eternity,
Beyond these shadows, where the soul would be
    Enraptured at the glorious heavenly sights.
He thought of this and them he'd leave behind
    To all the moil and duty of this life,
    Their future meeting, far from earthly strife ;
And, gazing on this arch, in his clear mind
    In time he saw the bridge lights to that shore
    Where pain, and death and sorrow come no more.

BELLE'S BABY.

A CHICK of ruddiest hue, a child of morn,
    Given to us when night was most away,
    Leaving its watcher, Venus, near the day,
To follow when the Light was fully born ;
    Thou art the prettiest baby come to earth,
A star of promise that may never set,
And full of possibilities to yet
    Bless and adorn the country of thy birth.
How thou 'rt caressed and crowed o'er every hour;
    How tenderly thou 'rt tended and perfumed ;
    Ne'er a colt so caparisoned and groomed,
Ne'er a parterre decked with a fairer flower.
    Why loved and fashioned so I cannot tell,
    Unless it is thou art the child of Belle.

HELICON.

A POET bound for distant Helicon,
　To quaff the nectar of its many springs,
A draft of which lays bare the soul of things,
O'ertook another deviously wandering on.
　Approving not such waywardness, he said :
"Straight have I come through jungle, city, mire,
Seldom my progress matching my desire ;
　The road seems long; how has thy journey sped!"
The other answered, " I have sought the field
　Where birds made melody, where flowers were
　　fair ;
While rock, and tree, and leaflet, sun and air,
Gave me new dreams not hitherto revealed."
　And thus each one thought his own road the best,
　While far away loomed Helicon in the west.

THE FALLEN LEADER.

WE placed him on a plane above the crowd,
　As he proved noble minded in the fight
Of equal rights for Ireland, as a right ;
And of his work and him—ay, we felt proud !
So deep our faith, we simply never thought
　That he possessed within his breast a heart—
　This Titan who made Ireland's enemies smart,
Whom every Irishman for help had sought.

'Twas pitiful he should stumble from that place ;
  Would that he had been wiser, for his foes
  Could use the lash on him with galling blows,
And, striking him, they did not help his race.
  So hard he worked when much he had to stem,
  Our eyes grow misty when we would condemn.

ON A POET WHO DIED YOUNG.

F. S. SALTUS.

HIS barque was wrecked near to the heights of
      Fame,
  And like a mist, on to another sphere
  He passed away, leaving behind him here
Thousands that knew him not, nor e'en his name.
Verse full of life and light, and never tame.
  He likewise left, rare gems that come quite near
  The Masters' works, those wonders that appear
Once in a hundred years for men's acclaim.
Short was his life, yet he developed powers
  So marvelous the whole world should regret
His early taking off.   What might we see
Had time been granted for such spiritual flowers
  To bloom aright?   Then men would not forget
Him now they know not ; but that cannot be !

MY HORSE.

MY horse I sometimes think of ; where is he ?
　　Companion in the war for many a day,
　His graceful, glossy flanks of Ruby bay,
His delicate head, with eyes that beamed on me
Good-naturedly and friendly, or in plea ?
　　Fleet-limbed and full of courage for the fray,
　　Enduring in the march, though long the way ;
Through hunger, dust and thirst ; where may he be ?
　I doubt he lives.　Myself am somewhat gray,
And man has twice the travel of a horse.
I'm glad I think of him without remorse,
　For kindly was he used in service long.
　I 'm glad we parted friends ; I heard his neigh
Over the peach field, like a farewell song !

A MIDSUMMER THOUGHT.

WE love this earth, somehow, if young or old ;
　　And though 'tis often censured, still 'tis ours,
　And though weeds multiply, it has its flowers,
With climates ranging wide from heat to cold ;
And he must lack the mind's true scope who can
　Go through all without a grateful thought
　At the concordant comeliness that's wrought
On sea and shore, mountain and plain, for man.

Sometimes I think that earth will ever keep
   Us chained unto its bosom, strangely wed ;
   That when unto dim eyes we may seem dead,
Our souls will still be active, not asleep,
   But living in the essence ; conscious, too,
   That 'neath us is the sward, and over us the blue.

RALPH WALDO EMERSON.

COULD I depict the marvel of thy lines
   I would be almost equal to thyself;
   So content I must be to admire thy pelf
Of Nature's coinage that thy skill entwines
Through all thy sayings, prophecies and pasts.
   Thy mind can claim equality with them,
The giant seers and poets, that like masts,
   Well rigged and sailed, are set 'twixt bow and
      stem
   On earth's great deck, inciting mankind on
To emulate their spreading sails of thought,
While breezes from the purer spheres are brought
   To swell the canvas, that the weak may con,
The strong wax stronger, the rose grow more red,
And the material man rise from the dead.

THE GALLANT ASTRONOMER.

I. D. J. SWEET.

EYEDEJA, poet, wit, astronomer,
 A great admirer of the moons of Mars ;
Sagacious—almost a philospher—
 Quick at repartee on street, boat or cars ;
One evening, lately, walking with some friends,
 Gazing intently on the starry skies,
Each planet's orbit at his finger ends,
 The light of knowledge in his eagle eyes ;
When pointing quickly upward struck the head
 Of passing beauty—"I beg pardon, Miss ;
Pointing out Jupiter, I find instead
 I have touched Venus ; censure not my bliss."
The lady blushed—was pleased—the stars looked
  down,
And for the life of them they could not frown.

THE INDIAN SUMMER.

THE fowler's shot resounds through pleasant air,
 The maples have put on their red and gold,
 The purple haze envelopes wood and wold,
And makes the homeliest things look soft and fair.
 The corn stands in the shock for winter's food,
The cows graze lazily along the stream,
The distant mountains now much nearer seem
 Than when the summer heats did o'er them brood,

The growing colt frisks gayly through the field,
  Nor thinks of toil in store for him and me ;
  A sluggish feeling calms our energy,
And makes the mind to dreamy fancies yield.
  The Indian summer has possession got
  Of all our thoughts and senses, and what not.

AT LAST !

LONG years he had been knocking at their door
    To gain admittance ; but no beggar he.
  For offerings he brought that well might be
Accepted by these censors of pure ore.
The temple keepers deemed his work a whim,
  Not sense with elegance for cultured eyes ;
  And from a distance eyed him, over wise,
As he grew old in waiting, pitying him.
The soul immortal of his toilsome life
  Could not be stilled or killed, but grew more
      bright
  As he approached the end, the death, the night,
And his last days with glorious thoughts were rife.
Alas ! that he must die the goal to win :
His statue, laurel crowned, they placed within.

IDIOSYNCRASIES.

A SOLDIER of the Cross once had a dream,
   After a battle, resting by a stream :
He saw, upon his way, an Infidel
With blood which flowed from wounds both deep
      and fell,
A hand quite powerless, and a dragging limb
That yielded but a burden sore to him,
Trying to reach the stream to quench his thirst.
The soldier felt like slaying him at first,
But drops like rain now falling from the sky
Caused him to turn a sudden glance on high ;
And in the blue—'twas clear—he saw a face
Bearded but lovely, with a divine grace,
Whose lips still smiled and spoke to him: "Oh spare
Thy brother ; what thou hast that let him share !"
And strange about the soldier it may seem
That when he woke he thought it not a dream.

INTERMISSION.

TALK is a pleasantness unto a meal,
   And laughter aids digestion, peal on peal.
It may be all within the realm of prose,
Or gossip, or improvement; or, who knows
But it may take a moral tone, and then
We get the higher standards of the men.

It may be rhyme, or rhythm, or poetry—
How easy on these three to disagree.
Of attic salt; ideas without rhyme,
And rhyme without the soul, a mess of chime.
It may be long-nosed Dante down below;
Or the quaint conscience Raven of poor Poe.
How old Don Quixote gave mankind such joy;
How Mr. Pickwick felt the Bardell boy—
But, greatest eaters will in time get full,
And too much gorging makes a tame man dull.

PROMETHEUS.

HE seems to be at liberty,
    Yet bound in potent chains is he
Who snatched the flame from off Jove's throne—
To bless humanity 'twas done.

They whom he stole it for ne'er come
To cheer his mountain martyrdom,
Where 'neath the ravening vulture's bite,
Silent he suffers day and night.

Nor cares he, knowing that mankind
Will not forever be so blind;
And even should his story die,
His fire has immortality.

O poet! lift thy torch, and wait;
Heed not the vulture thrusts of fate;
The world may heedlessly pass by,
But not a living thought will die.

Alike in crowds, or solitude,
Be evermore thy strength renewed;
Bear forward, be thou slave or lord,
The light which is its own reward.

OLDCASTLE.

OLDCASTLE, my sweet native village,
   That my eyes long so often to see,
My mind would receive its worst pillage
   If it could be deprived but of thee;
For there is not another on earth
   That can equal thee, home of my heart,
While the memories of joy and of mirth
   That surround thee shall never depart.

'Tis long since I saw thee, my birthplace;
   'Tis long years since I stood on thy green,
Ere wandering afar in this earth race—
   Yet, though far, far away have I been,
I feel that the brook is yet singing,
   The fair bluebells and cowslips to charm;
While birds o'er the meadows are winging
   As they did in my youth o'er Sky Farm;

That the fairies of Strawhan are dancing,
   Taking home frisky wights that are full;
That at Ruethaw the black dog's enhancing
   The ghost stories when evenings are dull;

That the Big River yet has its fishes;
 That Cornbawn's still a mountainous thing;
That the Head Inn yet has its blue dishes,
 And Love Lane still retains its pure spring.

But I wonder if on the play ground
 Have the boys the same games as when I
Was one of the crowd in that gay round
 Of the pastimes we all fain would try?
Ah! no; I suppose there are others
 Take the place of those now passed away—
More novelties for our young brothers,
 Giving joy and amusement to-day.

Yet oft when the twilight is falling,
 And the moon her pale crescent displays,
Kind memory within me's recalling
 To my mind those most earthly blessed days
And hope says I'll be on the morrow
 With the scenes and companions of yore;
But I wake from my musing in sorrow,
 For I know we may never meet more.

BIRTHDAY VERSES—A. W.

A LITTLE girl is seven years old to-day;
   Loved friends have come to see and make
   her glad;
In every tone of voice there is a play
   Conforming to the joy, while none are sad.
Enjoyment reigns, the festive hours fly by,
   Commemorating that the earth was blessed
When she came down from out God's Autumn sky,
   Here to remain and be its honored guest.

In fancy I can hear the music's chime;
   The dainty feast of goodies I can see;
The rushing and the rapture when play-time
   Expands itself 'mid youthful revelry:
My heart can feel it all and join the throng!
   O youthful hearts! God bless you every one!
Roll on their years, oh, Time, 'mid mirth and song!
   Each day like this we'll miss when it is gone.

THE UNITY OF MAN.

M AN cannot raise alone,
    More than can float a stone;
The environments of life
Bring him peace or bring him strife.
Though he strive with great desire,
In his burning heart of fire,
With his mind in wild delight,
In the selfishness of might,
To arise above his kin,
And to shun them in their sin,
With diseases of the town
That he would forever frown—
Ah! the wavelets of the air
Will convey them even there,
Where his palace lifts its head,
Where he rests on downy bed—
Ah! the passions of his brain
May there make his labor vain;
Or the outside world of thieves
May conceal beneath his eaves,
And when night is o'er the earth
May disturb him in his mirth;
And his talent and his gold
May not save him in his fold,
Nor secure his life-long lease,
Nor impart to him much peace;

For he'll find the low must rise
To the height of his own skies
Ere his heaven is secure—
Ere he ceases to endure;
For throughout all nature's plan
Is the Unity of Man!

AFTER THE BATTLE.

THE sun has vanished in the west,
  Leaving scorched plains and heights at rest,
While cooling breezes earth invest.

The twilight fades above the hill,
Where we to-day have fought our fill,
And where the enemy is still.

Fair Cynthia begins to throw,
From the soft crescent of her bow,
Her showers of silvery shafts below.

While hills and valleys, meadows, streams,
Lie beautiful beneath her beams,
Like pictures in a painter's dreams.

And hark! there comes upon the ear
The whip-poor-will's low note, so near,
So sadly sweet and coldly drear.

It throws a gloom upon the heart
More than could any song of art,
Giving the soul an inward start.

Ah, sad bird! mournest thou what is fled—
Something to which thy heart was wed?
Or is it for the battle's dead?

If for these dead, oh, sing away
Till morning comes, with streaks of gray
Upon his chariot's ruddy ray.

For they with heroes now belong,
And slain for right or slain for wrong,
Are worthy of the sweetest song.

Ah! must thy music cease so soon?
Faint and more faint thy low notes swoon,
Slow dying with the dying moon.

Perhaps upon life's checkered shore,
Where thought at least can upward soar,
Thy mournful voice we hear no more.

And yet methinks I hear thee still,
Lingering about yon distant hill—
'Tis fancy, not the whip-poor-will!

THE MOUNTED RIFLES.

IN 'Sixty-one and 'Sixty-two,
  We went into the fray :
From farm, from shop, from school, from mart,
  We donned the war array.
The Union was in danger, though
  Its foes, more brave than wise,
Did reck not of the Northern hosts
  That would in time arise.

Our little band, the Rifles, they
  Did ever well their part,
Whether in duty on the flank,
  Or to the foeman's heart ;
And, though they're few around us here
  To talk the record o'er,
Our standard never kissed the dust,
  But triumphed at the fore.

How well the olden names sound now
  Of daring fight and scout ;
They crowd into the memory,
  We would not keep them out ;
From Camp Hamilton to Richmond,
  Three years—to some 'twas four—
How many a mile we raided through
  Virginia o'er and o'er.

At Norfolk and at Providence Church,
  Carsville and Isle of Wight,
And Joyner's Ford, and Zuni, where
  We had full many a fight,
And Blackwater, old Blackwater.
  To there how many a ride—
'Twas at the bridge that Wheelan brave
  Was wounded ere he died.

The Dismal Swamp, and Suffolk, too,
  South Quay and Somerton ;
Gatesville, Hertford and Edenton,
  We've fought and had our fun.
The Deserted House and Franklin,
  Scott's Mills and Chuckatuck,
And Winton, and at Jackson, where
  We had the best of luck.

At Gloucester Point and Matthews's, and
  To King and Queen in vain.
With Kilpatrick, as avengers, to
  Where young Dahlgren was slain ;
And, if my memory fails me not,
  Sage Oberteuffer, too,
Near Warsaw fell in leading on
  His men—a soldier true.

And Williamsburg and Bottom's Bridge,
  And back unto New Kent.
And at Charles City Court House, where
  To victory we went ;
And Slatersville, Balt'more Cross Roads,
  And o'er to Jones' Ford,
And back near Fort Magruder, where
  The chills and fever bored.

Do you know Bermuda Hundred,
And Walthal Junction, where
That Beauregard came down at night,
But found his equal there?
And Procter's Creek, Wire Bottom Church,
And Drury's Bluff so high,
New Market Heights and Darbytown,
Where Freedenburgh did die.

And Petersburg, Deep Bottom, too,
And o'er to Chapin's Farm,
Up unto the Johnson House, where
We kept the flank from harm;
Then down to North Carolina, where
We cut the Weldon Road;
When Richmond fell and Lee was beat,
And cotton-fields were hoed.

Ah! how our hearts beat joyfully
That April morning fair,
When with banners soiled and tattered,
We camped at Capital Square?
We had reached at last the city,
The goal of all our aims,
The fort of the Confederacy—
Great Richmond on the James!

We did our part to end the war,
Success did crown our task,
And what was left of us came back,
In the sun of peace to bask;
Returning to our several homes,
Our ways begun anew,
Each with experience to keep
His duty well in view.

Twenty-five years have passed since then,
  And many are forgot,
Death from disease has conquered some
  The foeman's art could not :
And who can doubt these vanished ones
  Now reap what bravely sown,
And march, and guard, and picket lines
  To us as yet unknown.

O veteran ones !   O Riflemen !
  Let's not forget the past ;
Let's keep its memories fresh and green,
  So they shall surely last.
The Union's out of danger, but
  The men who fought the fight
Should never be allowed to starve,
  Or houseless be at night.

A parting toast I give you, ere
  Out in the night we go—
Not as of old to picket, or
  To scout, or fight the foe—
'Tis "Our Glorious Flag, God bless it !
  Long may it proudly wave ;
And soldiers of the Union rise,
  When danger comes,—to save."

GENIUS.

I ASKED three men I met one day
 What genius was?—their hairs were gray,
And much experience made them sage,
And they were bright lights of the age.
One said it was a "food from Heaven,
That came to some with extra leaven."
Another said 'twas "work, and will
To do and dare, and life fulfill."
The last one shook his hoary head—
"Genius is death"—'twas all he said.

Well, here we have three thoughts forsooth;
So tell me man, or hopeful youth,
Which of these three hath spoke the truth?
Or, is each one like to a stream
That images each living scene—
Thro' which it's moving in a dream—
Giving but to the voyager,
Be he poet or philosopher,
Whatever come before the eye—
Whate'er he sees in passing by.

Is genius then so very fine
Not to be measured by a line?
A something secret to mankind—
Outside the standard of the mind?
Beyond the compass, well-known rule—
Almost synonymous with fool—

Projecting thought, ideal, sublime
To live throughout the coming time ;
From Homer, with the Trojan War,
That lives tho' kings have gone ;
To Clarke that put " Night's mantle on,
And pinn'd it with a star."

NEVER UNKNOWN.

WHERE'ER they be, rich or hewers of wood,
　　Bound to a wheel for aspiring toward good,
Thirsting for things that fade ever away,
Building up hopes to come down every day ;
Be they well or ill, let them laugh or groan,
The gods to themselves are never unknown.

If they 're seated with Jove to eat and sup,
Or drink the lees from the tyrant's cup ;
If they dream Elysium's peaceful dream,
Or are shut in dungeons without a gleam,
They still have pleasures, however alone :
The gods to themselves are never unknown.

The wind may whistle, the storm may come on,
And the sun, the moon, and the stars be gone ;
The mind can survive, it has its own shore,
O'er which the ocean of death cannot roar.
Ye cannot deprive it of what's its own :
The gods to themselves are never unknown.

SWEET REST TO HIM !

SWEET rest to him, tender and bright,
　　Last mighty captain of our fight !
　His country owes him boundless praise
　For faithful service all his days,
With sword and brain true to the right.

When treason rose in deadly might
This gallant, fearless modern knight,
　　In duty sought the battle's blaze !
　　　Sweet rest to him !

In these last years, with hair grown white,
To see him was a pleasing sight.
　　Children were happy in his gaze ;
　　Women and warriors sought his ways ;
His gracious manners gave delight—
　　　Sweet rest to him !

A SON OF EARTH.

I DWELL within this world of din,
  Where they who work most chiefly win,
And where the people censure sin.
I mark the rose's timely fall,
I hear the robin's pensive call,
And I love God's children one and all.

I love to read the human thought
Which has in volumes been outwrought,
By poets who great Nature sought,
And philosophers and sages,
Whose ennobling thoughts and pages
Have come down with all the ages.

I love to hear the sublime cry
Of thunder, rumbling through the sky,
While lightning flashes quickly by.
I love to hear, brought by the gale
And falling on my roof, the hail,
Like strokes of strong man with a flail.

I love to see the downy snow
Cover the earth, while winds do blow
And sleighs o'er roads a dashing go.
I love to see the winter's fire,
While there sit youth and aged sire,
Telling the tales which all desire.

I love to see the morning hour,
When dew has jeweled leaf and flower,
Ere the Day-god displays much power,
While through the air the song bird's notes
Come warbling from a thousand throats,
And in my heart the music floats.

I love to feel the calm of eve,
When the western zephyrs weave
Cool garlands o'er the brows that grieve.
I love to muse throughout the night
And feel, though seeing not the sight,
The planets moving in their might!

I love to see earth's loving hearts
Joined in the love that ne'er departs,
Not linked in sordid moneyed marts—
Whether Mendelssohn's splendid march
Resounds through aisle and Gothic arch,
Or they are wed beneath the larch.

I love to see the hoped-for birth
Come glorified upon the earth,
While there are joy and healthful mirth.
I love to see the laughing child
Grow up, not tame nor over wild,
But blessed with intonations mild.

My kingdom is the love that I,
'Midst all life's shadows hovering by,
Would keep for all beneath the sky.
With love I'd reign, with love I'd win
All from the paths which men call sin—
All to the Light that dawns Within.

ALPHA AND OMEGA.

AN old man and a child, upon the strand,
  Severally look toward life's surging ocean:
The child, with light experience, will land
  His ships to-morrow; he has no notion
              That they to shore
              May come no more.

His are the eyes of hope—the radiant lens
  Bringing to his mind whate'er is cherished;
The old man, from a varied lifetime, knows
  That some of his treasured ones have perished—
              Were lost at sea,
              Howe'er hoped he.

The child, blessed one, has merely touched the
        brine;
  Life's voyage, storm and calm, is before him;
The old man's sailed—now nears the sunset line
  And shore that, God willing, will restore him
              His wrecked and tossed—
              His loved and lost.

"THE 79th HIGHLANDERS."

N. Y. VOLS., 1861–1865.

Written on receiving a copy of the above work by William Todd.

FRIEND Will: I've read your big, braw book,
  Your labor of love, that certainly took
You many years to think on;
And by all odds it is the best
Of regimental histories:—a bequest
  For its members well to prink on.

In spirit I've been with you all—
FromBlackburn's Ford, your early call,
  Until at Appomattox;
Mid weary marches, darksome days,
And battles, not all bringing bays,
  With salt-horse more than fat ox.

A gallant chronicle all way through,
With mirthful incidents which do
  Make it most interesting;
And he who says *his* regiment
Can match this record should relent,
  Or is but merely jesting.

What mighty names this record shows,
Where giant armies came to blows,

First Bull Run and Port Royal,
James Island and Secessionville,
  And Kelley's Ford, till fighting still
    Second Bull Run pleased th' disloyal.

Chantilly, South Mountain, Antietam—
The last two names which almost dam
  The stream of Fredericksburgh—
Green River Bridge and Blue Springs.
At Campbell's Station victory rings,
  With Jackson and Vicksburg.

At Knoxville where you nearly starved,
And at Fort Sanders where you carved
  Your names on the heights of fame;
At Strawberry Plains and Wilderness,
And at Spottsylvania where you press
  To that charge where victory came.

At Fort Stedman and at Hatcher's Run,
Where the Union Army almost won,
  And the Southern legions toss'd,
Till the morn when Petersburg fell,
The last chords of the rebel yell,
  Where the Southern cause was lost.

Well aided by your book I've been,
With you on march or camp-fire scene—
  Travel by rail or steamer—
Your debtor made in many ways.
May health and happiness bless your days,
  Is the wish of E. S. Creamer.

TAPESTRIES.

H ERE in the room where oft I sit,
    And where I weave my webs, or knit
The thoughts that come into the mind,
When the imagination's kind,
At times I'm startled at the way
Surroundings with one's thoughts have play.
Even the tapestry on the wall,
That days we hardly note at all,
Shows to one's moods a difference—
A something almost kin to sense—
Reflecting, like a looking-glass,
Much that within the mind may pass.

When the world seems to be my friend,
And nothing happens to offend,
The tapestry looks of pattern prim,
As if 'twould never show a whim ;
Of placid outline, debonair,
To breed contentment anywhere.
But let, instead, things go awry,
Which ever to avoid I try,
Fiends from therein look out at me,
And hold unnatural jollity,
Enlarging parts that hardly hint
Of form and face, and fleshly tint,
Into queer shapes that broadly grin,
And add unto what's ill within.

THE MODERN ARTHUR.

KING ARTHUR, he of the Cymric line—
　　Where have time's surges borne him now?
Where they who quaffed his generous wine?
Where she, the precious maid divine,
　　Whose health was drunk? whose winsome brow,
And voice, and luscious lips were toasted
　　Till nothing but the lees remained?
Yet still the gallant knights all boasted
　　That love, true love, could ne'er be drained;
　　　　For that was fed by fire
　　　　Made by the heart's desire;
　　　　And not e'en grim despair
　　　　Could quench its burning there.

Our Arthur lives to-day in town,
　　Who cares about his modern name?
His Round Table is loaded down
With wine that could the others drown.
　　His friends are wanting not in fame;
His daughter, whose bright form of beauty
　　Man never saw but would possess,
Could wake a hermit's mind to duty—
　　Whose health is drank with a caress.
　　　　The knights of old again
　　　　Would live, death's work in vain,
　　　　If brought but for an hour
　　　　Beneath her magic power.

BELLS OF MORNING.

EACH morning, as I lie in bed,
 I hear a far-off bell's sweet tone
Welcome the day gleams, rosy red,
 And telling me that night has flown.

So one, upon his dying bed,
 Hears bells of a celestial tone
Welcome the soul far overhead,
 And telling him that death has flown.

THEOLOGY.

WORSHIP of God is laudable;
 His truest name is audible,
 So that the spirit ear may hear.

Hell is the fitting recompense
Of uncouth actions, lacking sense,
 Stifling the laugh, causing the tear.

Heaven is the fruit of fruitfulness,
The answer of true life, to bless;
 Work and development are here.

MUSIC.

ALL things had reached creation, but stood still,
      Awaiting the divine creative sign
To move with life eternal ; and His will
   Chose music for the signal, gift divine!

"CHARGE THEM, BOYS!"

Last words of Captain Owen Hale, Company K, Seventh
United States Cavalry, killed fighting the Nez Perce Indians,
near Bear Paw Mountain, Sept. 30, 1877.

"CHARGE them, boys !" cried Captain Hale,
      When he struck the Nez Perces,
Who were hidden in a vale,
   Having been pursued for days.
Charged his men, and fired as well,
And a score of Indians fell.

      Joseph's band returned the fire ;
         Sent some volleys up the hill,
      With an art that did not tire,
         And a skill that seemed to kill ;
      But our boys, like gallant braves,
      Held the ground, tho' on their graves.

Fearless Hale got rifle wound,
   Which with soldiers' pride he'd hide ;
Cheered his men ; the next one bound
   Into his throat—breach made wide ;
Raised his arm, like foe to quell,
Uttered, "Charge them, boys !" and fell.

What can be a nobler death
   One can think, of 'neath the laws,
Than to give one's truest breath
   To support a nation's cause ?
Nations build upon such deeds—
Freedom lives where freedom bleeds.

"Charge them, boys !" will fire the age
   That is present, or to come ;
Add a courage to the wage
   When the bugle sounds and drum ;
And our land should bless the speech
That brings victory to its reach.

Would I sang a bolder note !
   Where all chords of life did teem,
Which for eras on might float,
   Married to so brave a theme ;
For a theme so worthy fame
Might enhance the singer's name.

Poets, in this age of gold,
   Wanting heroes—this is one !
Patrons of the true and bold,
   Raise the statue ! now he 's gone.
Long as valor shall prevail
Shall "Charge them, boys !" of Captain Hale.

SOMETIME, SOMEWHERE.

NE'ER tell us that all the endeavor
    We make shall bring fruitage never;
That there's no such place as heaven,
That sinnners cannot be forgiven,
That sin, like the wound on the finger,
May heal, but the scar will yet linger,
Nor vanish through years or tears.

The answer speaks never to doubt us,
Endeavor reaps harvests about us;
While happiness comes to the masses,
And fire may restore wilted grasses.
When wrong to the stubble-field 's righted,
It blooms as it ne'er had been blighted,
A meadow of fragrance for years.

JOHN HOWARD PAYNE.

His remains were brought over from Tunis, at the expense of Mr. Corcoran, of Washington, D.C., and were reinterred, with appropriate services, at the beautiful Oak Hill Cemetery, June 9, 1883.

BACK to the land that gave him birth,
    He 's brought to rest forevermore,
To mingle with his mother earth,
    Back from the far Tunisian shore.

Here we'll his sacred dust entomb,
  Beneath his own loved flag unfurled ;
But who could tomb his song ? 'Twill bloom
  Long as mankind live in the world !

What sailor, 'neath the stars or sun,
  Wherever he may chance to roam,
Or soldier, when the battle's done,
  But in his heart loves "Home, Sweet Home?"

The emigrants who leave the land
  That gave them and their kindred life,
The thousands landing on our strand,
  All love the song with home so rife.

Yet he who wrote it seldom could
  Claim that he had a home.   His song
To publishers brought fortunes good,
  While he with poverty lived long.

Now he is back unto his own ;
  A generous man advanced the means,
And after three decades have flown,
  His dust is mid familiar scenes.

Ah ! if his gentle spirit sees
  From the immortal homes on high,
Retaining yet his faculties,
  This does his soul much gratify.

Poor wanderer ! back to home again,
  To rest 'neath flowers and showers of June,
Thy simple song from simple men
  And women shall not perish soon.

Ah ! who'd not willingly bear much—
  Blessed in the fame so great as thine—
To strike the lyre with master touch,
  And make the song almost divine ?

Give thanks ! the road to heaven is free,
  And song to fame may yet attain ;
Away from years of poverty,
  Who conquers here ? John Howard Payne !

THE FILLED BEAKER.

AH ! the time that we spend on abstractions !
  With what is their study fraught ?
How we dream and revel on the future,
  That delusive dream of thought ;
And though water is drawn up in vapor,
  Returning again as rain,
What we pass in our lives without prizing
  May never come back again !

How we hunger and hope for bright visions,
  That rarely to us come near ;
How we long to gain desolate North-lands,
  That to reach we ought to fear,
While the great and enjoyable present
  We neglect, or even shrink,
Though its beaker stands filled on life's table,
  Inviting us all to drink !

A VILLAGE MAID.

MYRA hath beauties pleasant to behold ;
  Her silken crown 's adornment for a queen;
  Her eyes are windows where the soul is seen ;
Her mind 's a store of treasure, good as gold ;
Her heart is to be won, you say, not sold.

Never before beneath earth's arching skies
Was such enchantment in a maiden's eyes ;
  And yet she 's in the market to be sold.
Never was village maiden such a prize,
  Who bids ? Bid high, in love, not gold.

A LOOK AT THE POST.

ONE way or another
    This comrade and brother
Was not at our meeting,
Nor quaffed of our greeting,
Of our duty and cheer,
The best part of a year,
When he came in one night
And in evident delight,
An enjoyable host,
For to look at the Post.

He had fought in the ranks
And expected no thanks
When our land was in throes
Of its internal foes.
From the war he brought back
A sore wound, and alack!
A bad habit, to drink
More than useful, I think.
His old wound often pained,
So the goblet he drained.
And the pension he got
He misused—'twas a blot,
He had faults I confess,
And I would he had less.

He had hard years; disease
Got him down on his knees,
And for long on his bed
Lay his poor ulcered head;
But he rallied, got so
That about he could go,
Yet an omen, bequest,
Soon him prophesied rest,
And he felt, who knows why?
He was shortly to die;
And he went to the P'ost
To say " good-by," almost.

And the Post did compose
Of old soldiers, of those
Who braved hearts to the fire
Of the South; to the mire
Of its roads; to the ken
Of its prison and pen.

The old veteran all gray,
And the younger one gay,
Here assembled as friends,
To outwork friendly ends.

So his home he forsook
For to take a last look
Of the Post; of these men
He might ne'er see again.
Some had been near him South,
At the red cannon's mouth;
Ah, some two, or some three,
In the same company.
In his heart he cried, quite,
As he bade them good-night.

Afterwards soon to bed
He laid down his tired head;
And he suffered great pain,
Never rallying again.
He that braved many a raid
Was of death not afraid,
And he died (heaven him keep)
Like a child going to sleep.

Where's he camping to-night?
Ah! his soul may have sight,
And from yon spirit coast
Take a look at the Post.

SOME DIVINE STEPS.

THE essence of all things that dwells on high,
   To whom the human soul oft turns for balms,
  Lets downward to the earth, in storms or calms,
Steps which gives superb prospects to the sky,
And stimulate humanity to pry
   Into Divinity—its suns and fanes.
Homer, that glorious step, how grand to try
   And climb it ! From Dante's step e'en the plains
Of the departed can be kenn'd. Shakespeare's
   Shows diversity in entireness. Milton's
Shows scenes sublime. Goethe's in beauty rears,
   And lovely views give Burns and Emerson's.
The needs of souls find here and there a rise
   Of steps divine to help them to the skies.

BETTER THAN HE KNEW.

A BAD man in his garden found a weed
   That caused him trouble, so he thought he'd
   take
  And cultivate it, so that he might make
It more a source of misery by its seed,
   And thereby trouble neighbors, good and bad.
Much valued time he spent in labor hard,
Developing this thing in his back yard ;
   And when he deemed this noisome weed he had

Grown to perfection, as to smell and size,
  To injure much his neighbor's cheerful grounds,
  When night had spread her mantle on his rounds
He went, scattering its seeds.   To his surprise
  His culture had developed pleasing powers—
  Each plant grew up the home of fragrant flowers.

STORY'S SEMIRAMIS.

THERE in a modern city sittest thou,
    The queen that some four thousand years ago
Had built the walls of Babylon ; thy fair brow
  Crowned with Assyria's jewels ; a great foe,
And conquering princess, that brought 'neath thy
        sway
Persia and Egypt, and their mighty force,
And north to where Caucasus stood at bay,
  And east to where the Indus found its source,
Within the present age again thou 'st won.
  The Teuton, Anglo-Saxon, Celt and Dane,
And children of them all, a race begun,
  Acknowledge thy great powers, accept thy reign,
And crowd the portals of the courtly scene
Where, in thy wondrous beauty, thou art queen.

PRESUMPTION.

SINGING and playing on a charmed guitar,
　　Her graceful fingers, tapering and white,
　Thrilled all the strings, her voice at middle height,
Until the finch let loose his song to mar
　The waves of harmony, so much less sweet
His voice was than the lady's.　The proud bird
Doubtless grew jealous of the strains he heard,
　And sought her matchless cadences to beat.
Rash bird! thou rivalest a magic art;
　And though in truth thy song is sweet and fine,
　She can make simple melodies divine,
And lift to heaven the simple, longing heart.
　'Tis days since I have seen her, but her eyes
　Still thrill my heart with music soft and wise.

THE VISION OF THE SKULL.

WITHIN a dream I looked upon my skull,
　　Fleshless and white—I marvelled why 'twas
　　so—
　Leaving quite plain its convex, high or low,
Once with nerve tissue and thought fibre full.
　Some day shall I thus look upon my past,
Seeing the whys and wherefores of that time—
The causes predisposing mind toward rhyme—
　Toward imagery immortal, grand and vast?

Shall I there see the shackles of the mind,
  Those skull-chains which the brain has on the
      soul,
  Those birth gifts, which do keep it in control,
Which limit work and aspirations bind?
  Ah, shall I learn that, be we quick or slow,
  To knowledge by an effort must we grow?

ROBERT EMMET.

AGAIN thy welcome birthday has come round,
      O martyr saint of liberty for man !
Again within thy own loved land is found
  The struggle for thy hopes.   Another plan
Is working now.   The dungeon yet can keep
  The hero in its bosom ; the scaffold
Yet may have its victims, and we, too, can weep
  To see some wretched ones succumb for gold.
But when we look to thee, O mighty one !
  Our fears and doubts all vanish, noble heart,
That to the far-off spirit world hast gone.
  Still art thou in our efforts yet a part ;
Still art thou our incentor ; while our tears
Keep green the grass above thee through long years.

FAILURE.

FORGIVE my writing that thy beauty 's rare,
Though this the veriest fool might freely own;
Forgive me if I say that thou hast grown
So beautiful that no one need compare
Thee with past beauties or the modern fair.
All of all comeliest lines in thee is shown,
And this surpassing truth is not unknown
To those who magnify where I forbear.
But I will boldly write that the best
Of earth would vanish wert thou from it gone;
Naught else so lovely can the sun shine on,
And shadows dark would then engloom the heart.
But many, seeing thou art here and well,
Could all of this, and more, much better tell.

TO THE SHADE OF W. W.

THOU lover of the cosmos vague and vast,
In which thy virile mind would penetrate
Unto the rushing, primal springs of fate,
Ruling alike the future, present, past ;
Now, having breasted waves beyond death's blast,
New Neptune's steeds saluted, white and great,
And entered through the glorious Golden Gate,
And gained the fair celestial shores at last,

Still worship'st thou the Ocean? thou that tried
  To comprehend its mental roar and surge,
  Its howling as of victory, and its dirge
For continents submerged by shock and tide.
  By that immortal ocean now what cheer?
  Do crews patrol and save the same as here?

WARM DAYS IN DECEMBER.

THE warmth hangs o'er the naked, bare-limbed
      woods,
  Enmantling them in garments of blue haze;
And even the ruts made by the spring-time floods
  When that Apollo with his golden rays
Sent melted snow in runlets down the hills
  And watersheds, swelling the little streams
To treble their capacity of rills,
  Appear like ancient gold with ruddy gleams.
Some vigorous maples yet retain their leaves,
  Proud of their mottled dress of fading sheen;
And the slow-running brook his way yet weaves
  By fir and myrtle, and through sods yet green.
Some migratory birds in cosy nooks yet stray
Where sheltered glades abound and south winds
    play.

CHRISTMASTIDE.

PEACE and good will toward men ! Blest
    Christmastide
  That brings to famished thousands a good meal ;
  While even those immured in cells that steal
From others for a livelihood, now bide
  At tables loaded with the best of fare.
Children unused to luxuries and joys
Now have abundance, are e'en bless'd with toys,
  For did not Christ take such unto his care?
The laborer sick, his family hungry, cold,
  Is now remembered ; wood and coal, and rent,
  And flour and meal, and fowl to him are sent
By them that know the genuine use of gold ;
  Whose eyes have seen the shepherds watch by
    night,
  Or read the Sermon on the Mount aright.

ON THE HUDSON.

THE glow of perfect day unconscious lies
  O'er Hudson's wide expanse this autumn tide,
  When nature's banners, streaming far and wide,
Are mirrored in its waters with the dyes
Of Indian summer's painting—darks and brights—
  Enveloping the prospect, till we seem
  Wrapped in the splendors of an Orient dream.
O river ! whose soft waves reflect all lights,

By farm and palace where mankind may dwell,
Happier than by the Shannon, Thames or Rhine,
Could I have but a cottage to call mine
  On thine enchanting banks, it would be well ;
Where musing, from earth's tumults I'd be free
To watch thy peaceful journey to the sea.

EPILOGUE.

WE find them now within the land of dreams,
    Where Hope does often clothe the mind in
    gleams
Of what we'd most desire in waking hours,
When our best wishes would project our powers.
The Professor has at length his long sought boon;
O'er the Atlantic rides his great balloon.
The Soldier is a general, not content;
His friends now talk of him for President.
The Mechanic's heart is as light as cork;
Has just been chosen Mayor of New York.
The Minister now dries up many a tear;
An ample salary has he for each year.
The Doctor's well, with large estate secure;
Can give his service gratis to the poor.
The Lawyer is in Congress, sleek as mouse;
Has been elected Speaker of the House.
The Gambler's made a hit, and flown from strife,
Is settled now within the woods for life.
The Broker he has horns, has many gored;
Has been elected President of the Board.

The Merchant, in the waters seeking truth,
At length has found a spring which brings back
    youth.
The Driver has a wife, and wayside inn,
And friends yet come his services to win.
The Poet blooms in fame, is at his prime;
Has found a firm to publish every rhyme,
The Woman is a wife, with children four,
And a good husband who does her adore.
    And so we leave them, trusting that the day
Will no reaction bring to mar their play;
That the same fancy, which has cheered their night,
Will not forsake them when returns day-light.